"STRIKE OFF MY HEAD!"

Chup begged the Lady Charmian; then he turned and knelt down slowly, face toward the cliff. Charmian was at his right, holding the long blade point down at the ground. He said, "Now, about this little surgery I need ... I suppose a single stroke would be too much to ask for. But more than two or three should not be needed, the blade is heavy and quite sharp." Without turning to see her face he added, "You are the most beautiful, and most desirable by far, of all the women I have ever known."

From the corner of his eye he saw Charmian losing her hesitation, gathering resolve, straightening her thin wrists in a tight two-handed grip to lift the weapon's weight. Chup studied the details of the rock wall before him.

He had knelt down facing this way so that his head would not roll over—

Enough of that. He was Chup. He would not even close his eyes.

FRED SABERHAGEN

EMPIRE OF THE EAST, BOOK II

THE BLACK MOUNTAINS

THE BLACK MOUNTAINS

Copyright © 1971 by Fred Saberhagen

A Baen Book

Baen Publishing Enterprises
260 Fifth Avenue
New York, N.Y. 10001

First Baen printing, March 1988

ISBN: 0-671-65390-3

Cover art by Robert Stein III

Printed in the United States of America

Distributed by
SIMON & SCHUSTER
1230 Avenue of the Americas
New York, N.Y. 10020

EMPIRE OF THE EAST, BOOK II

THE BLACK MOUNTAINS

I

Tall Broken Man

The great demon came to Chup in the middle of an autumn night of howling wind. It came in the midst of a torrent of air, whose vortices rose seemingly within a single gasp or howl of attaining life; it came with a blast that shook Chup's hovel of a shelter, pitched against the inside of the Castle wall. Lying sleepless with the nagging of his ever-painful wound, for many nights, Chup had heard time and again the screaming passage of things that from their sound were on the verge of becoming elementals of the air. So it was that he paid little heed to the demon's first shaking of his lean-to.

But soon the shaking grew more violent. A prolonged pounding against one end of his little shelter bounced its crooked boards against the wall of enormous stones. Raising his upper body on his elbows, Chup looked down the length of his paralyzed legs in the direction of the sound. And he saw, like smoke flowing through the crevices of his patchwork dwelling, the demon coming in.

Involuntarily he stiffened. The thing from the East would have been his ally, in his days of power; what business it might have with him now he did not know. And even a strong man, thinking demons were his allies—even such a man, when a demon came to him at midnight, and at hardly more than arm's length distance, might know himself strong indeed if he resisted the urge to run, or to cover his eyes and flatten himself on the ground.

As for being able to run, Mewick's battle-hatchet

had seen to that. And as for covering his eyes — well, he was still Chup. Raised on his elbows, he kept his gaze fixed steadily upon the smoky image coalescing in the close space before him. Outside the wind moaned softly, relieved of bearing that which had come in to Chup. Rain began to spatter on the lean-to.

Inside the hovel, space changed and distance grew as the face of the demon began to take its shape. Chup could scarcely make out on it anything like a human feature, and yet he knew it was a face. As it became a little more distinct there grew in Chup the fear that he might understand what he was looking at, that at last he might perceive the features rightly and that when he did they would be too horrible to see.

Nothing but demons could shake him like this. Now his eyes demanded, if not closing, at least to be allowed to slide out of focus. With a sigh he at last let them do so.

Only then, as if it had waited for that token yielding, did the demon speak. Its voice was a skeletal hand, searching furtively through dead leaves: "Lord Chup."

The power tapped by this pronouncing of his name made its image plainer in his sight. With a shudder he gave up trying to face down the thing, and let himself sprawl back on his rude bed, a forearm flung over his eyes. "I am Chup. But Lord no longer."

"But Lord again, mayhap." The dry leaves rustled, stirred by finger-bones. "Your unclaimed bride, the Lady Charmian, does send you greeting now through me."

"A greeting — from where?"

"From her place of power and safety in the Black Mountains."

Of course, the demon could be lying. It could have come merely to torment a cripple, like some nasty child on a romp; sometimes no meanness was too small for them to bother with. But no, on second thought. It would not have come so lightly to this castle now, filled as the place was with an army of wizards and warriors of the West; even demons had to heed some dangers. It was here, then, on important business.

Without lifting his arm from his eyes, Chup asked: "What does my Lady want of me now?"

The image of the demon's face began to form inexorably inside Chup's eyelids, under his forearm that could not keep it out. Moving what did not seem to be a mouth, it said: "She wishes to share with you, as with one worthy of her, her present power and glory and delight."

Now whether he opened his eyes or shut them, the demon's face, like some hideous afterimage, remained the same. "Power?" Suddenly shaking-angry, Chup raised his head and glared. "Power is mine, you say?" His enemies had not heard a groan or a complaint from him in half a year, but now the fullness of his bitterness burst out. "Then show me that I have just the power to move my legs—can you do that?"

Below the monstrous face the darkness worked. There appeared a pair of hands, roughly manlike but deformed and huge. They were visible in the light that sprang out when a cover was removed from an object held in one of them. It was a large, thick goblet or bowl, dark itself but holding a bursting warmth of multicolored light. That glow ate away the darkness, and seemed to half-obliterate the demon's image, and yet it did not dazzle when Chup looked directly at it.

The demon's free hand reached for Chup. He uttered an involuntary grunt, but did not feel the repulsive contact he expected. There was only an impersonal force that spun his body halfway round. Now he lay face down, with his dead feet still pointed at the demon. On his back, right in the old unhealthy wound where Mewick's hatchet had bitten at his spine, Chup now felt a cold touch as of icy water. A moment later there followed something, some kind of shock, that might have been pain of terrible intensity but was ended so quickly that even the timidest man could scarcely have cried out.

When that clean shock had passed, Chup realized that it had burned away the nagging gnawing that had lived in the wound almost since it was made. Before he could think beyond that point, the next change came, a dazzling tingling down the great nerves of both thighs. Automatically he tried to move his legs. Still they would not stir; it was long months since those wasted, shrunken muscles had contracted, save for painful and uncontrollable twitchings. But even now he felt those muscles try.

With his arms he turned himself again upon his back. The demon, withdrawn slightly, was recapping the vessel from which it seemed to have poured his healing. Warmth and light vanished. Chup again faced only a distorted presence, dim in darkness. The only sounds in the hovel were those of rain and autumn wind, and Chup's lonely, ragged breathing that now gradually grew steadier.

"Is this a true healing?" he asked at length. And then: "Why have you done it?"

"A true healing, sent to you by your bride, that you may come to her."

"Oh? Why, then, she is very gracious." Chup could feel the coursing life down to his toes; he tried them, but they were still too stiff to move. He did not dare accept this miracle as true; not yet. "She is full of unexpected kindness. Come, messenger, I am no child. This is some prank. Or—what does she need me for?"

With the speed of a blow, the demon-face came looming over him. He was Chup—but he was no more than human. He could not, with all his will, keep from turning his head away and lifting up an arm as if to ward a blow. His stomach, that had never troubled him before a fight, now knotted in spasm.

His eyes clenched uselessly upon the demon-image looking through their lids.

Unhurriedly, the voice of dry leaves scraped at him. "I am not to be mocked, lord though you were, and lord you are to be. Not to be called 'messenger' in insolence. Much less shall you scorn those who sent me here."

Those? Of course, Charmian herself was no magician, to have the ordering of demons. She would again have charmed a wizard or two into helping her, with whatever scheme she played at . . . The demon would not let him think. He was to be punished for his disrespect. He had the sensation that the demon was starting to peel away the outer layers of his mind, with no more effort or concern than a man toying with an insect. They could change men. If it kept on it would turn him into something far less than a cripple. Unless they really needed him—he cried out. He could not think. He was Chup, but he could not stand against an avalanche.

"You are not to be mocked," he whispered, through clenched teeth. "Nor are your masters to be scorned."

The effortless onslaught faded. When he was master of his eyes again, there was nothing to be seen but the bearable dim face.

The demon then began impersonally to tell him why he was needed. "Among the forces of the West now gathering in this castle, there is a peasant youth named Rolf, born here in the Broken Lands."

There could have been more than one fitting that description, but Chup had no doubt who was meant. "I know him. Short and dark. Tough and wiry."

"That is his appearance. With him he now carries, always and everywhere, a thing that must be taken from him. It must be brought to the Lady Charmian—and to no one else—in the Black Mountains, and soon. When the youth goes into battle, what we seek may be destroyed or lost. Here the power of the West is too strong for me or any other to take the thing by force; stealth must be used.''

"What is it?''

"A small thing in size. A knot woven from a woman's yellow hair. A charm of the kind that men and women use when they seek from one another what some of them call love.''

Yellow hair. Charmian's own? He waited for the demon to go on.

It rasped: "Tomorrow your legs will bear your weight, and soon they will be strong enough for battle. You are required to get this charm before the Western army marches—''

"They may move any day!''

"—and bring it to your Lady. Men in her service will be patrolling in the desert, a few kilometers to the east, watching for you. Beyond that you must expect no further help.'' The hugeness of the demon's face was growing less; Chup saw how far the space beneath his slanting roof had stretched, now it was coming back.

The dry voice too was fading. "I will not come to you here again. Except to punish you for failure.'' And then the face and voice were gone, the hovel it had occupied was ordinary. The wind outside went howling loud again. Chup lay without moving until it had become an ordinary sound, burdened with no more than the rain.

The rain and clouds delayed first entry of the morning's light into the long and crowded barrack-room. When Rolf woke all was still in darkness, round him the familiar jumble of packs, equipment, weapons, and bunks and hammocks with their load of snoring bodies.

He who had roused him, without touch or word, stood at the foot of Rolf's bunk, a tall and bulky figure in the gloom.

"Loford? What—'' And then Rolf guessed what

had brought the wizard to him. "My sister? Is there something?"

"There may be. Come." Loford turned away. Rolf was into his clothes and had caught him up before Loford reached the door.

The wizard turned to a stair, and as they climbed the rising turns of stone toward the Castle roof, he explained in a low voice: "My brother has arrived. He is speaking much of technology and how we may be able to use it. Of course I mentioned your experience, and your handiness along that line, and he was interested. I told him also how I have tried with my poor spells to learn what happened to your sister. Beside my brother I am a backwoods dabbler. Certain powers that I never could have commanded, he has called up and set to work. Understand, the answer we get may be incomplete, or . . ."

"Or may not be one I want to hear." They were starting up the last steep stair, leading to the battlemented roof of what had been Ekuman's private tower. "Still I thank you. It will not be your fault if the news is bad."

Emerging on the roof, Rolf pulled his jacket tighter against the dying drift of rain, and through habit, without thinking, made sure that something in an inner pocket was safe. Mist hung like wet garments round the tower, and no sentry had been posted here in this hour before the dawn. Near one battlement a tripod supported a brazier in which glowed a green, unearthly-looking fire. Besides the fire a motionless figure in wizard's robes stood looking out away from the Castle, into the rainy night.

Loford raised one finger to his lips, gave Rolf a warning glance, then led him forward. The green fire flared up once, the waiting figure turned, tall and spare. Hood and shadow concealed the face of Loford's brother. His fingers moved as if he tested some invisible quality of the air. Arrayed on the paved roof around him, Rolf now saw, were some of the things that good magicians used: the fruits and flowers of autumn, what looked like water and milk in little jars, small heaps of earth and sand, plain wooden twigs, some bent, some straight. The green unsteady light had changed them all, but they looked innocent and simple still.

The hooded figure beckoned, with a turning of its head, and Rolf went to stand beside it, still keeping silence as he had been signed to do. Now, looking out across the battlement into the east wind and its drifting rain, he saw the clouds and tendrils of lethargic mist speed faster past him. In a moment it seemed to Rolf that he stood on the prow of a racing ship of stone, driving into a gale. A vase holding flowers was blown in from the parapet, to land at Rolf's feet with a tiny smash.

Rolf put out his hands to grip the stone before him. The man beside him raised a long arm, pointing nearly dead ahead. Just at that point the driving mist flew faster still, became a gray smooth blur that was not mist, and then tore soundlessly from top to bottom. Rolf peered into the opening, leaned into it, and then for him the wind and rain were gone. A vision engulfed him while it seemed that he hung bodiless in space.

A forest clearing, that he had never thought to see again. A house of thatch and poles, simple and small, the garden, the familiar path, fowl in a pen beside the house. The vision was utterly silent, but it held life and movement, sun and shadow shifting with a breeze. Then in the shaded doorway a dim figure moved, one hand with a gesture that Rolf had seen ten thousand times wiping itself on his mother's familiar ragged apron.

Rolf cried out then, as in a nightmare, knowing and enduring the worst before it happened. And someone, disembodied too or at least invisible, was gripping his arms, speaking with Loford's kind whisper in his ear: "It is all written! All unchangeable! They cannot see or hear you. You can only watch, and learn.''

His mother had shaded her eyes, looking out; then she stiffened with alarm, hurried inside, and shut the useless door. Rolf did not know how he could keep watching. But he had no choice. He must learn Lisa's fate. And he must learn who *they* were, the ones who came. Soldiers of the East, of course. But Rolf wanted their faces and their names.

In the foreground of the vision now the first of them appeared, a mounted trooper wearing black and bronze, his back to Rolf. Behind him came another and another, the beginning of a line. There were six of them in all. Their mouths were wide, with soundless shouts or laughter, their weapons were held ready. And now the door was opening, Rolf's mother standing there again.

A time came presently when Rolf could no longer look. He shut his eyes and floated in a void, but could not flee the thought of what was happening. At length there came what must be Loford's hand, large and unseen, to clamp his chin and shake his head gently, trying to force him now to see.

The hut had already been contemptuously kicked to bits. The bodies of his mother and father were hidden in its small ruin, for the son to find when he came running home. Here was Lisa, twelve years old, long hair still neatly bound up in peasant style but her garments torn and smeared, her face as pale and blank as death, hoisted awkwardly up before a soldier's saddle. Wiping blades and straightening clothing, the marauders were almost ready to leave. He who carried Lisa must be their officer, for he alone wore half-armor, and he rode the tallest steed. Now as he turned his mount out of the yard toward the road, he showed Rolf his youthful, unlined, and harmless-looking face. There was a soft, proud, almost pouting look about the mouth.

If she were seriously injured, dying, they would

not have bothered carrying her off. " . . . alive?" So choked was his throat, Rolf had to try twice before he could speak intelligibly. "Is she alive now? Will I find her?"

Loford, at a little distance, murmured something, and Rolf understood that his question was being passed on. Then Loford brought back an answer, which he whispered to Rolf slowly, like one who did not understand the message he conveyed: "She lives. You must get help from the tall broken man."

"What? Who?" This time there was no reply. Rolf drifted, bodiless and alone. "Then what of those who took her?" he demanded. "There were six. How many of them still breathe?"

The vision changed. Rolf now beheld a portion of a simple, unpaved road, running through green, wooded land. Rolf recognized the spot as one near where his home had been.

A trooper in black and bronze came riding into Rolf's field of view. Gone were his cheeks and eyes and nose, and his jaws of weathered bone gaped wide, showing missing teeth. What might have been dried leather clung in fragments to his skull and to his skeleton's hands. Rolf understood that he was answered regarding this man's fate.

The second mounted trooper hove into view. He grinned, for he too was a skeleton, although it seemed he had good grounds for peevishness. Straight before him there extended the long handle of a farmer's pitchfork, long tines vanishing in his tunic's front, and coming out his back as fine, sharp points. Rolf had one third his answer now.

The third wore flesh upon his bones, and breathed, but only in a vision could anyone so wasted sit on a beast and ride. His scalp was marked by an old wound, his eyes rolled vacantly. The fourth man came, a handless skeleton: had he survived his maiming, and fled with other of Ekuman's people to the East, there to discover no one could be bothered feeding him? The fifth man rode past jauntily, a hatchet buried in his fleshless skull. The over-throw of Eastern power in the Broken Lands had taken heavy toll.

The tallest beast came last, with Lisa still carried unconscious before the saddle. She lived—but Rolf saw with a shock that she was changed. Her body looked the same, and her ragged garments and her dark-brown, bound up hair. But her face had been transformed, from its familiar homeliness to beauty that awoke an echo from Rolf's dreams and made him catch his breath. This was the girl whom he had called his sister, yet it was not. He called her name out, once, and then fell silent, marveling.

Her captor, too, was live and whole. His full-fleshed image with its proud, bored face watched indifferently the ghastly capering before him of his slaughtered men.

"Does he live, then?" Rolf demanded of the air.

He will be slain and he will live, he thought the answer came.

"Loford?" The vision was suddenly spinning before Rolf like a reflection in a whirlpool. He staggered, drew in a deep breath, and found himself firmly in his own body once more, standing on the solid Castle stone. Loford and Loford's brother were close beside him, and the light of day had come, to make the green fire ghostly dim. The last torn ribbons of the fog were swirling far above them now, borne by what seemed no more than a natural wind.

A wizard's or a statue's face, that of Loford's brother, lined but somehow ageless, loomed over Rolf. "Call me Gray," the statue said. "You will understand I cannot casually use my real name. How is it with you?"

"With me? How would it be? Did you not see?" Then Rolf felt Loford's grip upon his arm, and fought to calm himself. "I am sorry. I give you thanks, and ask your pardon, Gray."

"I grant it," Gray said solemnly.

Rolf turned from one of the wizards to the other.

"She lives, then. But where? Tell me, could he still have her with him? The one who took her?"

"I do not know," said Gray. "You heard the only guide that we were given to further information: 'get help from the tall broken man.' I expect that will prove decipherable to you. I am not sure what powers we reached today, but at least they were not definitely evil, and I would tend to trust them. Though they were strange . . . it seemed to me I spoke with one who held the lightning in his hands . . ."

A little later, Rolf stood on the tower alone save for the sentry who had come with day to scan the desert. While he was deep in thought, gazing out over the complex crowded courtyards of the castle, Rolf saw a familiar figure by the newly rebuilt main gate in the outer wall, dragging crippled legs out of a beggar's lean-to.

A broken man, who once was tall.

When it had become apparent that Chup was not going to die, he had been placed under close guard by the new masters of the land. Thomas and other leaders of the West had come many times to question him. Chup had told them nothing. They had not tried to force answers from him; new to revolution and to power, they probably were not sure what questions needed answers, nor what information Chup was likely to possess. Probably he could not have told them much of any use. He knew little of Som the Dead, of Zapranoth the Demon-Lord, and of the Beast-Lord Draffut, the powers of the Black Mountains, two hundred kilometers distant across the desert. They were the powers that the folk of the Broken Lands and the other newly freed satrapies must fear, and must eventually defeat if they were to retain their freedom. Unlike most others of his rank in the Eastern hierarchy, Chup had never formally pledged himself to the East, never passed through the dark and little-known ordeals and ceremonies. He had never visited the Black Mountains.

A few of the Free Folk, as the successful Western rebels in the Broken Lands did sometimes call themselves, had perhaps been willing to show some mercy to a fallen enemy, at least to one who had never been known to dabble in pointless cruelty himself. Perhaps for that reason Chup's life had been spared. Chup himself thought it more likely that after the physicians and the wizards had looked many times at the ill-healing wound on his back, had jabbed pins and burning sticks at his useless unfeeling withering legs, and had decided that no herb nor surgeon's knife nor wizard's spell could ever mend what Mewick's flashing hatchet-blade had severed, then the Free Folk of the West were quite content for him to live. Existence as a cripple among enemies might well be thought a punishment worse than death.

So they let him go, or rather one day they dragged him out of the cell in which he had been guarded. Explaining nothing to him, they simply dragged him out and walked away. When he was left alone, he used his hands to drag himself on. When he got as far as the great new gate where the road came in through the massive outer wall, he could see the empty distances the road ran to, and found no point in trying to crawl on.

When Chup had been sitting for half a day beside the gate, preparing himself to starve, there came one he had never seen before, an old man, to leave beside him a chipped cup with some water in it. Having set this down as if he were doing something shameful, and hardly looking at Chup, the old man walked quickly on.

Thinking it highly unlikely that anyone would trouble to poison him in his present state, Chup drank. Somewhat later, a passing wagoneer, perhaps a stranger, looked down from his high seat, perhaps saw only a beggar instead of a fallen enemy, and tossed Chup a half-gnawed bone.

Chup propped his torso erect against the castle wall and chewed. He had never been too finicky about his food when in the field. Turning his head to the right, he could squint across two hundred kilometers of desert to a horizon darkened by the Black Mountains. Even if he could somehow get there, the East that he had served had little use for the crippled and the failed. That was of course quite right and realistic, fitting with the way the world was made. Where else? A few kilometers to the west was the sea, to north and south, as here, his former enemies were in power.

The village just below the Castle was in ruins from the fighting, but people were already moving back and rebuilding. The road here promised to be a busy one. It seemed that if he must try to live on handouts he was not too likely to reach a better place than this.

By the night of that first day he had gathered scraps of wood and had begun to build his lean-to near the gate.

On the morning after the demon's visit, Chup had life back in his legs. Before emerging from his shelter he had tested them, gritting his teeth and laughing with the glorious pain of freely coursing blood and thawing muscles. Whatever the source of the healing magic, it was extremely powerful. He could bend each knee slightly, and move all his toes. His fingers told him that the wound upon his back had shriveled to a scar, as smoothly healed as any of his other battlemarks.

Now he must earn what the East had given him. He knew them too well to think for a moment that the demon's parting threat of punishment for failure had been an idle one.

Emerging at the usual hour from his shelter, he took care to give no slightest sign that anything of moment had occurred during the night. The light drizzle was fading as he dragged himself to his usual station at one side of the great gate, which had just been opened for the morning. As usual, he held in his lap his beggar's bowl, chipped pottery salvaged from a dump. His pride was too great to be destroyed by taking alms; it had been easier because he had never been forced to really beg. The weather had been good, and food plentiful throughout the summer. People came to look at him, a lord humbled, a villain punished, a terrible fighter beaten. People whom he never asked or thanked put in his bowl small coins or bits of food. There were no other beggars at the gate, and not many in the land. Western soldiers maimed in the fighting were still being cared for as heroes, and the others of the East, of less importance than Chup, had evidently been slain to the last man.

Sometimes people came to gloat, silently or loudly, at his downfall. He did not look at them or listen. They were no great bother. The world was like that. But he was not going to give them the satisfaction of dying, starving, or even showing discomfort, if he could help it.

Often it was the soldiers, even those who had fought against him, who gave him food and drink. When they spoke to him civilly he answered them in the same way. Daily he dragged himself to get water at their barracks well.

This morning, Chup had hardly taken his place beside the gate, when he saw the youth Rolf pacing across the outer courtyard toward him. Rolf stepped quickly but deliberately, frowning at the puddles, evidently on serious business. Yes, he was coming straight toward Chup. The two of them had not spoken since Chup was a Lord and the other a weaponless rebel. This visit today could not be coincidence; the demon must have somehow arranged it. Chup's chance was coming sooner than he had dared to hope.

Rolf wasted no time in preliminaries. "It may be you can tell me something that I want to know," he began. "About a matter that is not likely to mean anything to you, one way or the other. Of course I'll be willing to give you something, within reason, in return for information."

Not for the first time, Chup found himself somewhat taken with this youth, who came neither bullying the cripple nor trying to be sly. "My wants these days are few. I have food, and little need of anything else. What could you give me?"

"I expect you'll be able to think of something."

Chup almost smiled. "Suppose I did. What must I tell you in return?"

"I want to find my sister." Speaking rapidly, saying nothing of his sources of information, Rolf described briefly the time and circumstances of Lisa's vanishing, her appearance, and that of the proud-faced officer.

Chup scowled. The tale awoke real memories, a little hazy though they were. Better and better, he would not have to invent. "What makes you think that I can tell you anything?"

"I have good reason."

Grunting in a way that might mean anything or nothing, Chup stared past Rolf again as if he had forgotten him. He must not seem eager to do business.

The silence stretched until Rolf broke it impatiently. "Why should you not help me? I think you no longer have any great love for anyone in the East—" He broke off suddenly, like one aware of blundering. Then went on, in a slower voice. "Your bride is there, I know. I didn't—I didn't mean to say anything about her."

Here was a peculiar near-apology. Chup looked up. Rolf had lost the aspect of a determined, bitter man. He had become an awkward boy, speaking of a lady in the manner of one who cherished secret thoughts of her.

Rolf stumbled on. "I mean, she—the Lady Charmian—couldn't be harmed in any way by what you tell me of my sister or her kidnapper." One of Rolf's big hands rose, perhaps unconsciously, to touch his jacket, as if for reassurance that something carried in an inner pocket was safe. "I know you were her husband," he blurted awkwardly, and then ran out of words. He stared at Chup with what seemed a mixture of anxiety, hatred, and despair.

"I *am* her husband," Chup corrected drily.

Rolf came near blushing, or did blush; it was hard to tell, with his dark skin. "You are. Of course."

Though Chup preferred the sword, he could use cleverness. "I am so in name only, of course. You came breaking in the Castle gates before Charmian and I could do more than drink from the same winecup."

Rolf looked somewhat relieved, and utterly distracted now, despite himself, from whatever his original business with Chup had been. He sat down facing Chup. He wanted, needed, to ask Chup something more, but it took much hesitation before he could get it out.

"Was she really . . . I mean, there have always been bad things said about the Lady Charmian, things I can't believe . . ."

Chup had to conceal amusement, a problem he had not faced in quite a while. He managed, though. "You mean, was she as evil as they say?" Chup looked very sober. "You can't believe all that you hear, young one. Things were very dangerous for her in the Castle." Though not as dangerous as they were for others, living with her. "She had to pretend to be something different than what she truly was; and she learned to dissemble very well." Rolf was nodding, and seemed relieved; it amused Chup to have answered him with perfect truth.

"So I have thought," said Rolf. "She seemed so . . ."

"Beautiful."

"Yes. So she could not have been like her father and the others."

Of course, Chup thought, suddenly understanding the boy's monumentally innocent stupidity about the Lady Charmian. He was befuddled by the love-charm that he carried; the same that Chup would have to carry, later. However, time enough then to cross that bridge . . .

Rolf was saying, more calmly: "Nor were you, I think, as bad as Ekuman and the others. I know you were a satrap of the East, oppressing people. But you were not as vile as most of them."

"The most gracious compliment I have enjoyed in some time." Chup rubbed a flea-bitten shoulder against the cool, damp stone of the sunless wall. The moment seemed favorable for getting down to business. "So, you would like me to tell you where your sister may be found. I can't."

Much of Rolf's original businesslike manner returned. "But you know something?"

"Something that you'll want to hear."

"Which is?"

"And, since you are in earnest, I will tell you what I want in return."

"All right, let's hear that first."

Chup let his voice fall into a grim monotone. "If I can help it, I do not want to die like this, rotting by centimeters. Give me a rusty knifeblade, so I can at least feel like an armed man, and take me out into the desert and leave me there. The great birds are gone south on their migration, but some other creature will find me and oblige me with a finish fight. Or let thirst kill me, or a mirage-plant. But I am loath to beg myself to death before my enemies." It came out quite convincingly, he thought. Yesterday, there would have been more truth in it than fiction.

Rolf frowned. "Why must it be the desert, if you can't bear to live? Why not here?"

"No. Dying here would be a giving in, to you

who've made a beggar of me. Out there I'll have gotten away from you."

So long did Rolf sit silent, pondering, that Chup felt sure the bait was taken. However, the fish was not yet caught. Chup volunteered: "If you want to make sure of my finish, bring along a pair of swords. I think the chances would now be somewhat in your favor. I'll tell you what I can about your sister before we fight."

If Rolf was outraged by this challenge from a cripple, he did not show it. Once away from the subject of Charmian, he was adult again. Again he was silent for a time, watching Chup closely. Then he said: "I'll take you to the desert. If you lie to me about my sister, or try any other sort of foolishness, I won't leave you in the desert, dead or living. Instead I'll drag you back here, dead or living, to be displayed beside this gate."

Chup, keeping his face impassive, shifted his gaze into the distance. In a moment Rolf grunted, got to his feet, and strode away.

II

Duel

———◆◆◆———

In midafternoon Rolf came back, leading a load-beast. The look of the animal suggested it might be a reject from the Castle stable that could not be expected to give useful service in the coming campaign. Slung on it were several containers that might hold food and water. Rolf had also armed himself, but not with two swords. A serviceable sword and a long, keen knife hung from separate belts cinched round his waist.

The time since morning had tested Chup's patience to the limit. First, of course, because he was not sure his fish was wholly caught. Secondly, the urge to move his legs had become almost overwhelming. Under his ragged trousers their muscles were far looser, and even seemed thicker, than they had been yesterday. The ache and tingle of returning life had turned into an itch for movement.

Rolf said nothing but halted his feeble-looking animal just beside Chup. Then he came to catch Chup under the armpits, and with wiry strength heave his half-wasted frame erect. The gate sentries turned their heads to watch, as did some passersby. But no one seemed to care if Chup departed. He was a prisoner no more, only a beggar.

Once standing, Chup gripped the saddle with his strong hands and raised himself, while Rolf guided his dangling legs into the stirrups. Rolf asked: "Are you going to be able to hang on, there? I wouldn't want you to fall and split your head. Not just yet."

"I can manage." Chup had forgotten how high

riding raised a man. Rolf took the loadbeast by the bridle, and they were off, down the sloping switch-back road that led first to the village and then the world.

Rolf walked with long strides beside the load-beast's head: a position that let him keep the corner of one eye on Chup. Chup, .for his part, breathed deeply with the joy of seeing the Castle gradually recede behind him, and the greater joy of surreptitiously testing his legs in the stirrups and feeling them respond.

Before they reached the village, Rolf turned off the road. He led the animal down a slope of wasteland to the beginning of the desert. The autumn day had cleared, and had grown almost hot. Ahead of them, gently rolling flatness shimmered with mirage. Sparsely marked with vegetation, it stretched on to the horizon, where towered the Black Mountains, jagged and enigmatic. Rolf had chosen the only direction which led quickly to solitude, and was heading straight east from the Castle.

Men in the service of the Lady Charmian were to be patrolling in the desert. That might or might not mean some help for Chup. He could not count on any.

Neither Chup nor Rolf spoke again until the Castle had fallen nine or ten kilometers behind them. At this distance it plainly overlooked them still, from its perch on the low flank of a mountain pass. But the eastward of this point where they now were, the lay of the land was such that a man going east could take advantage of declivities and brush, and perhaps never see the Castle or be seen from it again.

Here Rolf stopped the beast, and, still warily holding its bridle, turned to Chup. "Tell me what you know."

"And after that?"

Touching a water bag slung on the animal, Rolf said: "This I'll leave with you, and the knife. The beast goes back with me, of course. You won't be able to get anywhere, or to stay alive out here for very long, but that's what you asked for."

Chup was curious. "How do you plan to judge whether or not what I tell you is the truth?"

"You have no cause to seek revenge on me in particular." Rolf paused. "And I don't think you lie just for the sake of lying; do harm just for the sake of doing it. Also, I already know, on good authority, a few things more than what I've told you about what happened to my sister. Whatever you tell me should match with that."

Chup nodded several times. He had intended anyway to tell Rolf the truth; he could almost regret that Rolf would not live long enough to benefit.

"The name of the man you want is Tarlenot," Chup said. "He served as an escort commander and a courier between the Black Mountains and outlying satrapies. He may still; whether he still is alive I have no idea."

"What did he look like?"

"His face, as you described it. I've heard that women found him handsome, and I think he shared their view. He was young, strong, of middling height. An uncommonly good fighter, so I've heard."

"And when did you see him last?" Rolf might have had his questions on a written list.

"I can tell you that exactly enough." Chup turned his face to the north, remembering. "It was on the last night of my journey southward from my own satrapy, coming here to the Broken Lands to take my charming bride.

"I came on river barge down the Dolles, escorted by two hundred armed men. Tarlenot, with five or six, going northward, met us on the last day before we reached the Castle. He and his troop, being so few in unfriendly country, were glad to spend the night in our encampment."

"Who or what was he escorting then?" Rolf, listening eagerly, leaned forward. But he was not near enough, as yet, for Chup to lunge at him.

"He was escorting no one. Perhaps he carried messages. Anyway, he had with him one captive girl who might have been your sister. As nearly as I can recall, she must have been about twelve years old. Dark-haired, I think. Ugly. Whether she had any closer resemblance to yourself I can't remember."

"True, she was not pretty," Rolf said eagerly. He shook his head. "Nor was she my blood relative. What happened then?"

"I had other things to think about. I remember Tarlenot, if I am not mistaken, saying something about selling her, in the north. There was a tavernkeeper up there at a caravanserai—" Chup stopped, caught by a sudden thought. "Why, it comes back, now. On that night I dreamt, and it was most odd. I thought I wakened, while all the men in the encampment, even the sentries, lay sleeping all around me. Tarlenot rose up from his blankets, but I could see his eyes were closed and he was still asleep."

"What happened then?" Rolf was utterly intent, but none the less alert. And still no closer.

Chup thought he might better have kept quiet about the dream. It must sound like some devious lie or stalling tactic. But now he had begun it.

"I dreamt there came one from outside the firelight, taller than a man and dressed in full dark armor that hid his face and all his body. A great Lord, certainly, but whether of East or West I could not say. The earth seemed to sink down beneath his feet, as stretched cloth would yield to the weight of a walking man. He stood before the sleeping, standing Tarlenot, and stretched out his hand toward— yes, toward where the girl must have been lying.

"And the dark Lord said: 'What you have there is mine, and you will dispose of it as I wish.' Those were his words, or very like them. And Tarlenot

bowed, like one accepting orders, though his eyes
remained closed in sleep.

"Then all became confused, as in dreams it often
does, you know? When I awoke it was morning. The
sentries were alert, as they must have been all
through the night. The girl was still asleep, and
smiling. That recalled to me my dream, but then I
forgot it again in the press of the day's business."
The dream had been very vivid, and the way he had
forgotten and then remembered it was odd. Quite
likely it had some magical importance. But what?

Chup asked: "The girl was not blood relative, you
say? Who was she?"

"I call her my sister; I thought of her that way."
Seeing how intently Chup leaned forward, gripping
the saddle, Rolf went on. "She was about six years
old when she came to us, the year I was eleven. The
armies of the East had not yet reached here, but they
were in the country to the south, and people fleeing north sometimes passed along our road. We
thought Lisa must have come from some such group
passing through. My parents and I woke up one
spring morning to find her standing naked in our
farmyard, crying. She could remember nothing, not
her name or how she'd got there. She could hardly
talk. But she had been well fed and cared for up till
then; my mother marveled that she had not a bruise
or scratch."

"You took her in?" Chup would find out all he
could from the young fool. Before he should come
close enough . . .

"Of course. I told you, that was before the East
had come upon us; we had food in plenty. We
named her Lisa, for my true sister, that had died as a
baby." Rolf scowled, running thin on patience.
"Why are *you* questioning *me*? Tell me what happened to her."

Chup shook his head. "I told you, what happened
to her finally I do not know. Except for this: when we

separated in the morning, Tarlenot spoke no more
of going north and selling his captive, but of going
east to the Black Mountains." Weary of talking,
Chup reached for the waterbag and got a drink.

After probing Chup with his gaze for a time, Rolf
nodded, "I think, if you were making up a lie, you
would make one that was more satisfying and be-
lievable." And yet Rolf hesitated. "Come, if this tale
just now was a lie, tell me. The water and the knife
will still be yours. And freedom, whatever it may be
worth to you out here."

"No lie. I've done my part of the bargain, told you
all I know." Chup gripped his left leg with his hands
and pulled it free of the stirrup, and then the right.
He made them dangle lifelessly. "Come, get me
down. Another moment or two, and this animal will
fall beneath my weight."

"Swing yourself off with your arms," said Rolf.
"I'll hold its head."

Chup, had he been honestly trying, might not
have been able to manage getting off without using
his legs. Whichever side he lurched toward, one of
his limp legs hooked over the saddle, while the
other dangled awkwardly in such a position that it
was likely to be broken under him if he just let go
and fell. Even a man seeking to be left alone in the
desert to die would not like to start his ordeal with a
broken ankle. The beast grew restive, while Rolf held
its head.

At last Rolf muttered impatiently: "I'll lift you
down." Still holding the bridle with one hand, he
stepped to the side of the animal opposite from
where Chup was clinging at the moment. He freed
Chup's leg so it would slide easily over the animal's
back. Then, bridle still in hand, he moved back
around the loadbeast's head.

He found Chup standing free.

Rolf's moment of surprise was time enough for
Chup to half-lunge, half-fall, upon his victim. Chup

learned in that first moment that his legs were still far from their full strength. They could do little more than hold him up.

But they had served him well enough for a moment, and that moment was enough. Rolf's hand had moved quickly, but still he had hesitated fractionally between drawing sword and dagger, and by the time his choice had settled on the shorter blade it was too late. Chup's hand was there to grip Rolf's wrist and argue for the weapon. Grappling as he fell, Chup dragged the other down upon the sand.

The youth had wiry strength, and two good legs. He writhed and kicked and struggled. But already Lord Chup had the grip he wanted, on Rolf's dagger arm. Rolf's tough arm muscles strained and quivered, fighting for his life; the Lord Chup's brutal power, methodical and patient, wore them down.

The captured arm began to bend. It was near the breaking point before its hand would open and give the dagger up. Chup caught the weapon up, reversed; he did not want to kill Rolf until he had made absolutely sure the charm was still with him. If it was not, Rolf would have to tell him where it was. He clubbed Rolf along the skull with the butt of the knife, and Rolf went limp.

Inside Rolf's jacket, in an inner pocket buttoned shut and holding nothing else, Chup found the charm. No sooner had his fingers touched it than he snatched them back. When he took it, would it work on him as it seemed to have on this young clod? Turn him misty-eyed and doting over the treacherous woman whom he had wed for nothing but political reasons?

Only briefly did he hesitate. If he would be a Lord once more, he had no choice but to take the charm into his possession and carry it to the East.

The loadbeast, decrepit and lethargic as it was, had run off a few strides and was still stirring restlessly. Chup called to it in a soothing voice. Then he muttered the three brief defensive spells that

sometimes seemed to work for him—he was a poor
magician—and drew the coil of hair out of Rolf's
pocket.

It was an intricately woven circlet of startling
gold, large enough to fit around a man's wrist. Chup
had no immediate feeling of power in it, but obviously it was no mere trinket; it was not dull or
crumpled, though an oaf had kept it in his pocket
perhaps for half a year, and had probably given it
much secret fondling.

Chup did not doubt for a moment that it was
Charmian's hair. It brought her beauty sharply to
his mind, and he stood up, swaying on his reborn
legs, gazing at the charm. Aye, his unclaimed bride
was beautiful. Whatever else was said of her, no one
argued that. Charmian's was the beauty, made real,
that lonely men imagined in their daydreams. He
recalled now the ceremonies of their wedding.
There had followed half a year of death, for him. But
now he was a man again . . .

Eventually he took note of Rolf's stirrings at his
feet, and tucked the charm into a pocket in his own
rags, and bent to put an end to his victim. On Chup's
still-unsteady legs it was a slow bending. Before he
could complete it, one of his victim's feet was
hooked behind his right ankle, and the other came
pushing neatly at the front of Chup's right knee. The
warrior-lord had no more chance of remaining upright than a chopped-through tree.

When he landed on his back he lay still briefly,
raging at his own foolishness while he pretended to
be stunned. Pretending did no good, for the peasant
was not fool enough to jump on him. Instead, Rolf
was crawling and scrambling away, dazed-looking,
but also plainly full of life. Chup struggled erect,
and tried to hurry in pursuit. But instead of lunging
and pouncing he could only stumble on his traitor-
ous legs and fall again.

Quickly he was up once more, holding his captured dagger. But Rolf too was now on his feet,

sword drawn and pointed more or less steadily at
Chup's midsection.

Something he had almost forgotten began to grow
in Chup: his old happiness of combat. "At least," he
observed, "you have learned how to hold a blade
since last we fought."

Rolf was not minded to talk or even listen. His face
showed how he, too, raged at himself for carelessness. He lunged forward, thrusting. To Chup, his
own response seemed horribly slow and rusty; but
still his hand had not forgotten what to do. It came
up of itself, bringing the knife in an economical
curve to meet the sword. The long steel sang, shoot-
ing two centimeters wide of Chup's ribs. Then
quickly the sword slid back, to make a looping swing
and cut. Chup saw it was coming downward toward
his legs. They had no nimbleness to save themselves. He let himself drop forward, reaching down
with his short blade to parry the stroke as best he
could. He caught the sword blade in the angle between hilt and blade of his dagger, caught it and
tried to pin it to the ground. But Rolf wrenched the
sword away again. Rolf feinted twice before he
struck again, but there was not much skill in his
pretense, so Chup had time to get back on his feet,
parrying the real cut even as he rose.

Chup saw as they circled that the loadbeast was
moving steadily away. No help for that. His eyes
were locked on Rolf's, and both of them were breathing harshly. So it went on for a little time, with
nothing said. Rolf would advance and strike, or
sometimes only feint. Chup parried, and faked attacking in his turn. With his short blade he could
not very well attack a sword, held by a determined
foe. If Chup had had his strong legs he could have
tried and might have won—skipping back when the
sword cut at him, driving forward then at the pre-
cisely proper instant for striking. Without perfectly
dependable legs it would be suicide.

A first-rate swordsman in Rolf's place would have driven in on Chup, trying to stay just at the distance where the sword could strike but the dagger could not, pounding one stroke upon another until at last the shorter blade must miss a parry. Though Rolf was dangerous with a sword, he was far from masterly. Chup watched and judged him critically. Rolf was evidently determined he was not going to be tricked again into rushing to too close quarters with the Lord Chup. So he stood just a fraction of a meter too far away before he struck; and he failed to press his attacks. Against his efforts the knife in Chup's hand could, with a minimum of luck, stand like a wall of armor.

At last Rolf drew back a further step, and dropped his sword point slightly. Perhaps he hoped to provoke Chup into something rash.

But Chup only dropped his own arms to his sides and stood there resting, panting honestly. His legs were stronger than when the fight had started, as if exercise were an aid to the demon's magic. But in the joy of fighting, with health and strength and freedom come again, he had no great wish to kill.

He said: "Youngster, come with me to the East. Follow and serve me, and I will make you a warrior. Yes, and a leader of warriors. You may never be a great one with the sword, but you have the guts, and if you live long enough you may absorb a little knowledge."

The murderous determination frozen in the young face did not thaw for an instant. Instead, Rolf closed again, and struck, once, twice, three times, with greater violence than usual. The blades rang, rang, rang. Ah, Chup thought, it was too bad, a good man wasted as an enemy. Chup would have to kill him.

If he could. The desert this near the castle must be patrolled. Should a squad of Western cavalry appear, that would be all for the Lord Chup and his ambition and his golden bride. And, too, the sun was lowering. Suppose they kept on duelling here until nightfall? To fight with blades in darkness was more like rolling dice than matching skills.

Rolf circled round him now, struck less frequently, and appeared to be thinking more. It seemed that he was searching for the proper way, trying strategies in his mind. He might hit on the right one. He would have the guts to try it if he decided it was best. Chup therefore had better get the initiative, and soon. How? He would dare Rolf, anger him, play on young impatience.

"Come here to me, child, and I will impart a little knowledge. Just a little spanking is all that I intend. Come, no reason for you to be so much afraid."

Rolf was not even listening. He was looking eastward now, past Chup's shoulder, and there was a change toward desperation in Rolf's face.

Chup carefully backed up a step, to insure against surprise, and took a quick glance behind him. A thin cloud of dust rose from the desert, a kilometer or more away. Beneath the dust he glimpsed movement as of riders; and he thought that the riders were garbed in black.

Rolf, too, thought that he saw black uniforms, and plainly they were coming from the east.

Chup had lowered his blade again, at the same time stretching himself up to his full height. His beggar's rags were suddenly completely incongruous. In a lofty and distant tone, he said: "Burrow into the sand, young one."

Rolf's thought, like a cornered animal, jumped wildly this way and that. It would be hopeless, in this barren country, to try to run from mounted men. The approaching riders now seemed to be coming straight on, as if they had already spotted Chup, at least. He stood quite tall and willing to be seen.

"Don't be an idiot. Hide, I say."

Bending low, Rolf scrambled around the nearest

hummock, threw himself down there, and dug himself as rapidly and thoroughly as possible into the sand between two straggly bushes. Not much more than his head, emerging amid roots and wiry stems, was left unburied when he ceased his work and froze, hearing hoofbeats nearby.

Looking out over the top of the hummock, he could see the head and shoulders of Chup, who stood facing away from Rolf with chin held high. And in that moment Rolf felt a chill brush over him, a shadow unseen by eyes yet deeper far than any simple lack of light. Something enormous and invisible brushed by him, something that he thought was searching for him. It missed him, and was gone.

The many hoofbeats, their makers still unseen by Rolf, had halted. Dust came drifting above Chup. Now an unknown, deep, and weary voice called out: "And are you Chup? The former satrap?"

"I am the Lord Chup, man."

"Where is it? Were you able to—?"

Chup in his best commanding voice broke in: "And your name, officer?"

For a moment the only sound was the shifting of hooves. Then the deep tired voice said: "Captain Jarmer, if it makes any difference to you. Now quickly, tell me whether you—"

"Jarmer, you will provide me with a mount. That beast you see wandering away there will not support me longer."

Some of the mounts shifted their positions, and now Rolf could see the one he took to be the captain, scowling down at Chup. Mounted beside the captain was one in wizard's robes of iridescent black, with the hump of some small beast-familiar showing under the loose robes at the shoulder. The wizard juggled something like a crystal in his cupped hands. A facet of it winked at Rolf, with a sharp spear of the lowering sun; again he felt the sense of something searching passing by.

Chup in the meantime was continuing his debate

with Jarmer: "Yes, I have it, and it is not your job to ask for proofs of anything, but to escort me. Now the sooner you provide me with a mount, the sooner we will be where all of us want to go."

There was a murmuring of voices. Chup vanished from Rolf's view, to reappear a moment later, mounted. "Well, captain, are there any more problems I must solve before we can be off? A Western army lies within that fortress, and if they've eyes they've seen your dust by now."

But still the captain tarried, exchanging glances with his wizard. Then he spoke to Chup once more, in the tones of one who knew not whether to be angry or obsequious. "Had you no companion on your way out here from that castle? My wise man here says his crystal indicates—"

"No companion that I mean to tarry for. That ancient loadbeast, mirages, and a skulking predator or two." Unhurriedly, but ending all delay, Chup turned his new mount to the east and dug his heels in.

The captain shrugged, then motioned with his arm. The wizard put away his jiggling piece of light. The sound of hooves rose loudly for a moment, then rapidly declined, with the settling of the light dust they had raised.

Almost unbelieving, Rolf watched and listened to them go. When the last sound had faded he pulled himself out of the sand and looked. The riders' plume of dust was already distant in the east from which the night was soon to come. Turning back to face the castle, he saw that some sentinel had—too late—given the alarm. A heavy stream of beasts and men, a mounted reconnaissance-in-force, flowed from the main gate toward the desert.

Rolf stood there numbly waiting for them. He had been given back hope for his sister's life, but robbed of something whose importance he had not understood until it was taken from him . . . though in truth his feelings were more relief than loss, as if an aching tooth had been pulled. His hand returned again and again to the empty pocket. His head ached from the robber's blow.

Ask help of the tall broken man. Why had Gray's powers told him that?

III

Valkyrie

On the first night of the long flight into the east there had been only brief pauses to rest. During the following day their toiling across the enormous waste of land seemed to bring the Black Mountains no closer. Jarmer during daylight slowed down the pace somewhat, pausing for long rests with posted sentinels. Chup at each stop slept deeply, lying with his golden treasure beneath his body, where none could reach it without waking him. When he awoke he ate and drank voraciously, till those of the black-clad soldiers who had been ordered to share provisions with him grumbled—not too loudly. His legs grew stronger steadily. They were not yet what legs should be, to serve the Lord Chup properly, but he could stand and move on them without expecting to fall down.

The second morning of the journey, the sun was very high before it came in sight; the Black Mountains of the East were tall before them now, casting their mighty shadows many kilometers out upon the desert. Clouds draped their distant summits. Seen from this near, they were no longer black, nor particularly forbidding. What had given them the hue of midnight from a distance, Chup saw now to be the myriad evergreen trees that clothed the middle slopes like blue-green twisted moss.

The troop now traveled upon a long, slow rise of land by which the desert approached the cliffs. The chain of peaks ran far on either flank to north and south, and curved ambiguously from sight in both directions, so Chup was hard put to guess how far the range might stretch.

Straight ahead was one of the higher-looking peaks, sheer cliffs rising to its waist. Now from somewhere on the tableland above the cliffs it disgorged a dozen or so flying reptiles. Down to inspect the mounted troop they flew, on laboring slow wings; the air here must be high and thin for them, and the season of their hibernation was approaching.

Looking more closely at the cliffs as he rode ahead, Chup saw that they were not after all a perfect barrier. To them and into them a road went climbing, switchback after switchback. Toward that road and half-hidden pass Jarmer was leading his men. And indeed the frayed-out start—or ending—of that climbing road seemed to be appearing now, beneath the riding-beasts' hurrying hooves.

Chup was observing all these matters with alert eyes and mind, but with only half his thought. A good part of his attention was focused inward, upon a vision that had grown in his mind's eye through the two long nights and single day upon the desert.

Charmian. The weight of the knot of his wife's hair, swinging in his pocket as the wind and motion of the ride swung his light and ragged garments, seemed to strike like molten gold against his ribs. He remembered everything about her, and there was not a thing that made her less desirable. He was the Lord Chup again, and she was his.

The gradually steepening slope slowed down the tired riding-beasts. The road they traveled, empty of all other traffic, veered abruptly away from the cliffs, then toward them again, on the first winding of the steep part of its ascent. The cliff tops must be a kilometer above their heads.

Chup drank again from the borrowed waterskin he had slung before his saddle. His thirst was marvelous; the water must be going, he thought, to fill out his recovering legs. Their muscles still seemed to be thickening by the hour, though the speed of recovery was not what it had been at first. He stood up in his stirrups now, and squeezed the barrel of the beast beneath him with his knees. The skin on his legs ached and itched, stretching to hold the new live flesh.

On the next switchback the road climbed past a slender, ancient watchtower, unmanned on this road where scouting reptiles perched and the defenders above held such advantage of position. In Chup's mind the slender tower was an evoking symbol of the slenderness of his bride. Again, with another turning of the road, the riders passed shabby, dull-eyed serfs at labor in a terraced hillside field. Among them were a few girls and women young enough to look young though they labored for the East; but Chup's eyes passed quickly over them, only searching for one who was not there, who could not be.

Oh, he knew what she was like. He remembered everything, not just the incredible beauty. But what she was like no longer seemed to matter.

It was a long and arduous climb, up through the narrow pass. As soon as they had reached the top, men dismounted wearily, and animals slumped to their knees to rest. They faced a nearly horizontal tableland, rugged and cracked by many crevices. Across this wound the road they had been following, and at its other side, two or three hundred meters distant, sprawled the low-walled citadel of Som the Dead. Several gates stood open in the outer rampart of gray stone. It did not look particularly formidable as a defense. There was no need for it to be; a few earthworks, now unmanned, stood right at the head of the pass where Chup and his escort had stopped. It needed no shrewd military eye, looking back and down from here, to see that a few men here could stop an army.

Beyond the citadel, the mountain went on up, to lose its head at last within a clinging scarf of cloud.

This mountain, unlike most of those surrounding, was but little forested. Above the citadel, the rock itself grew black. The more Chup looked up at that slope, the better he perceived how odd it was. On that dark, dead surface—was it perhaps metal, instead of rock?—there were a few tiny, even blacker spots, that might be windows or the entrances of caves. No paths or steps led to them. They might be reptile nests, but why so high above the citadel, already at an altitude where the leatherwings had hard work to fly?

Jarmer was standing beside him now, looking forward as if half-expecting some signal from the citadel. Chup turned to him and asked: "I suppose that Som the Dead dwells there above the fort, where all the signs of life are gone?"

Jarmer looked at him oddly for a moment, then laughed. "By the demons! No. Not Som, nor demons either. Quite the opposite. That's where the Beast-Lord Draffut dwells—you may meet him one day, if you're lucky." Then worry replaced amusement. "I hope you're what you claim to be, and what you bring is genuine. You seem quite ignorant . . ."

"Just bring me to my lady. Where is she?"

Shortly they were mounting up again. Jarmer turned away from the largest gate, and chose a path that followed close beneath the wall, round to the south flank of the citadel. There a small gate was open, just wide enough for the troop to enter in a single, weary file. They dismounted in a stableyard, giving their animals into the care of quick-moving, dull-eyed serfs.

Scarcely had Chup got his feet upon the ground when there came hurrying to him a man with the indefinable air of the wizard about him. He gave this impression more powerfully by far than the one who had accompanied the patrol, though the newcomer had no iridescent robes and no familiar on his shoulder. He was slight of build, with a totally bald head that kept tilting from side to side on his lean, corded neck, as if he wished to view from two angles everything he saw.

This man caught Chup's ragged sleeve, and in a rapid low voice demanded: "You have it with you?"

"That depends on what you mean. Where is the Lady Charmian?"

The man did something like a dance step in his impatience. "The charm, the charm!" he urged, with voice held low. "It's safe to speak. Trust me! I am working for her."

"Then you can take me to her. Lead on."

The man seemed torn between his annoyance and satisfaction at Chup's caution. "Follow me," he said at last, and turned and led the way.

A series of gates were opened for them, first by black-garbed soldiers, then by serfs. With each barrier they passed, the aspect of their surroundings grew milder. Now Chup followed the wizard along pleasant paths of flagstones and of gravel, across terraces and gardens bright with autumn flowers and fragrant with their scent. They passed a gardener, a bent-leg cripple with a face like death, pulling himself along the path upon a little cart, his implements before him.

The last barrier they came to was a tall thorny hedge. Chup followed the bald wizard through a gateless opening. They came upon a garden patio, built out from a low stone building, or from one wing of it; Chup could not see how far the house extended. Here was the grass thicker and better cared for than before, and the flowers, between a pair of elegant marble fountains, brighter and more numerous.

By now the sun come round the mountain's bulk. It made a flare of gold of Charmian's hair, as she rose from a divan to greet her husband. Her gown was gold, with small fine trimmings of dead black. Her grace of movement was in itself enough for him to know her by.

Her beauty filled his eyes and nearly blinded him.
"My lady!" His voice was hoarse and dry. Then he
remembered, and regretted, that he stood before
her in the rags and filth of half a year of beggary.

"My husband!" she called out, in tones an echo of
his own. Mingled with the tinkling of the fountains,
it was her voice as he had dreamed of it, through all
the lonely nights . . . but no, he had not dreamed
of her. Why not? He frowned.

"My husband. Chup." The very sunlight was not
brighter nor more joyful than her voice, and in her
eyes he read what all men want to see. Her arms
reached out, ignoring all his filth.

He had taken three steps toward her when his
feet were pulled out from under him and a rough
gravel path came up to strike him in the face. He
heard a shriek of laughter and from the corner of his
eye saw a dwarfish figure spring up and flee away
from a concealing bush beside the path, trailing
howls of glee.

The unthinking speed in his arms had slapped
out his hands in time to break his fall and save his
chin and nose. Gaping up now at his bride he saw
her beauty gone—not taken away, or faded, but
shattered in her face like some smashed image in a
mirror. It was, as usual, rage that contorted her face
so. How well he knew that look. And how could he
have forgotten it?

She glared at him as he regained his feet. She
screamed out her shrewish filth and hate—how
often he had heard it, in the brief days he had known
her before their marriage ceremony. He had not
been the target, then, of course; she would not then
have dared.

Now why was she screaming all this abuse at him?
It neither hurt nor angered him. He had no inten-
tion of striking her or shouting back. She was his
bride, infinitely beautiful and desirable, and he
would have her and she must not be hurt. Yes, yes,

all that was settled. It was simply that this side of her character was annoying.

She was screeching at him. "—Filth! Carrion! Did you ever doubt I would repay you triply for it?"

"For what?" he asked deliberately.

A vein of anger stood out in her lineless forehead. For a moment she could not speak. Then, in a choking voice, not unlike a reptile's caw: *"For striking me!"* A tiny drop of spittle came far enough to strike his cheek, the touch of it a warm and lovely blessing.

"I struck you?" Why, that was mad, ridiculous. How could she think—but wait. Wait. Ah, yes. He remembered.

He nodded. "You were hysterical when I did that," he said, absently trying to brush the dust from his rags. "I did it for your good, actually. I only slapped you with my open hand, not very hard. You were hysterical, much as you are now."

At that she cried out with new volume and alarm. She backed away toward a doorway that led into the building. From a gap between hedges there came running three men in servants' drab clothes. One of them was quite large. Together they ran to make a wide barrier between him and his lady.

"Take him away," she ordered the servants in a soft and venomous voice, regaining most of her composure. "We will amuse ourselves with him— later." She turned quickly to the bald wizard, who was still hovering near. "Hann. You have made sure he has it with him, have you not?"

Hann tilted his head. "I have not yet had that opportunity, my lady."

"I have it," Chup interrupted them. *"Your* lady, wizard? No, she's mine, and I have come to claim her." He stepped forward, and saw with some surprise that the three fools in his way stood fast. They saw only his dirt and rags, and perhaps they had seen him fall when he was tripped.

He scorned to draw his knife for such as these. He

heeled an ugly nose up with his left hand, and swung his fist into the stretched-up throat; one man down. He grabbed a reaching hand by its extended thumb, and broke one bone with one wrenching snap. He had only one opponent left. This third and largest fellow had got behind Chup in the meantime, and got him in a clumsy grip. But now, with his fellows yelping and thrashing about in helplessness, the lout realized he was alone, and froze.

"I am the Lord Chup, knave; let go." He said it quietly, standing still, and he had the feeling that the man would have done so if he had not feared Charmian more than Chup. Instead the big slave cried out hoarsely, and tried to lift Chup and throw him. They swayed and staggered together for a moment before Chup could shift his hips aside and snap a fist behind him, low enough for best effect.

Now he was free to turn once more to claim his lady. She once more howled for help. The wizard Hann hauled out a short sword from under his cloak—evidently feeling his magic had turned unreliable with the onset of violence—and threw himself between Chup and his bride. But Hann was not the equal of the last swordsman Chup had faced, and Chup was stronger now than then. Hann dropped his good long blade and fell down screaming, when he felt the knife caress his arm.

This time, however, Charmian did not resume her noise-making, nor did she try to flee. Instead she stood with bright eyes smiling past Chup's shoulder. He heard a foot crunch gravel behind him on the path.

It was Tarlenot who stood there. He had already drawn his sword, at sight of the lawn littered with writhing, groaning men. His eyes lighted unpleasantly in recognition as Chup turned round to face him. Tarlenot was not a tall man, but powerful and long of arm. His short pink tunic showed bare legs as muscular as Chup's had been in his days of full strength. Around his thick neck was clasped a thin

collar of some dark, plain metal, a strangely poor-
looking thing for one to wear who was otherwise
garbed luxuriously. Tarlenot's face was haughty
now, more so than Chup remembered; the countenance of a pouty child grown big and muscular; his
fair hair fell with a slight curl round his ears. He
nodded his head lightly in recognition to Chup, and
gave him a little smile. But he made no move to
sheathe his sword.

"Tarlenot," said Charmian's ethereal and tender
whisper. "Make this one a gardener for us."

Chup bent and picked up the sword dropped by
the wizard Hann, who still sat moaning, bleeding
lightly, on the flagstones. The sword seemed stout
enough, though its twisted fancy hilt was not much
to Chup's liking. It did feel better than it looked.

"That is no gardener's tool," Tarlenot observed.
"And here we do not need another lord."

Charmian giggled quietly. "Tarlenot, his legs have
grown too straight. Bend his knees for him. We will
get him a little cart, and he will tend our flowers."

Chup sighed faintly and moved a step farther
from his lady. It was hard, when the woman you
were devoted to might stick a knife between your
ribs. She was his bride, and the only woman he
wanted, but there would be no trusting her.

"Tarlenot," he called, waiting while the other
made up his mind. "One questioned me about you.
Only a few days ago."

"Oh? In what connection?" The mind had been
made up. "First, though, would you rather I only cut
your tendons, or took your legs clean off? They say
that useless limbs are worse than none at all. You
should know, is it so?"

"He was one who meant to do things to you that
you would not like." Chup stepped slowly and easily forward. "Now he will never have his chance."
His legs were working very well, but he could have
wished to give them their first real test in practice.
He raised his blade as he advanced, and Tarlenot's

sword came up in a motion quite gentle and controlled, and with a careful metal touch the duel was joined.

With the first preliminary touches and feints Chup knew that he had met a formidable enemy, and one cautious enough not to be deceived by Chup's scarecrow appearance into taking the scarecrow lightly. And when Chup had to make a really quick hard parry for the first time, he realized there was no great endurance left in his own body, long underfed, but newly healed, and just finished with a long ride.

Tarlenot was fresh and vigorous. Had it not been for the residual effect of the healing elixir—fading now, though the good work it had done remained—Chup might have been quickly beaten. His muscles were left aching and quivering by two or three exchanges at full power and speed.

They circled slowly on the gravel path and flagstones, and felt for cautious footing amid the flowers between the tinkling fountains. Chup as he turned saw Charmian pass within his range of vision; he saw her with a gesture stay her other attendants, now running up, from any interference. He saw how bright her eyes were, and the expectant parting of her perfect lips. She would take the winner, but only to use him and discard him when it was to her advantage or merely suited her whim. Chup knew that, if Tarlenot perhaps did not. But she was Chup's . . .

And then in front of her face came Tarlenot's. "Let me see," said Tarlenot, "if I can hit the old wound on your spine, within a finger's breadth. How was it done? Like this?" And he attacked.

Chup parried desperately, and riposted; his weary arm thrust wide. "Not like that, no," he said. "But with some skill." Demons and blood, but he was tired.

And Tarlenot knew it. He was now carefully making sure that Chup's tremulous near-exhaustion was no sham. Now that Tarlenot had measured Chup's reach and something of his style, he began to push the fight harder. Harder, till he himself began to puff.

Now Chup gave ground steadily as they circled. Sheer desperation kept him going, now. He might back into a corner . . . he saw before him the gardener on his cart, with lifeless eyes . . .

No, he was the Lord Chup, and he would win or die. And just then Tarlenot's sword came flicking in a little faster than before. Chup saw the danger but his weary, tardy arm could not make the parry quite in time, and he felt the hot bite of the wound along his side.

With that hurt there came before Chup all the blackness of the past half year, all of it seemingly alive before him in the person of his foe. The hurt was rage, the rage was fuel, the only hope and power he had left. He let his fury drive him forward, striking fast and hard, stroke after stroke—and then he staggered, halting. He feigned a final exhaustion before his ultimate reserve of energy was quite gone. Tarlenot, with triumph too early on his face, came thrusting in as Chup had thought he would. Chup parried that thrust and spent his final strength in one last blow, straight overhand, cleaving downward at the angle of his enemy's shoulder and neck.

The sword touched glancingly the blackish metal collar, and then bit down through garments, flesh, and bone. He saw Tarlenot's eyes bulge out, and the red fountain leaping from the wound. Clear down to the breastbone Chup's sword smote, and Tarlenot was driven to his knees, and then fell backward dead, his arms flung wide.

Chup found the strength to set his foot upon the ruined tunic that had once been silken pink, and wrench to get his swordblade free. He staggered back, then and got his back against a wall. He leaned there choking while the world grew gray and dim before him with the throbbing of his heart, as if it were his own blood puddling up the walk.

But he was not bleeding much. His searching fingers told him that the cut along his side had parted little more than skin.

Charmian . . . but she was gone. That was all right. Let her play any game she wanted, but he was going to have her now. As soon as he had rested for a bit. A sound made him turn. A small mob of lackeys were goggling timidly at him from a distance. The odd sound did not emanate from them. From where, then?

Straight up. A flying reptile had emerged from one of the windowlike openings that marked the mountain's dead black upper slope. It was winging down toward where Chup stood—but not on reptile's wings, he realized. Its rounded, headless body, dead and rigid, considerably bulkier than a man, hung beneath a speed-blur such as the wings of hummingbirds drew in the air. But this blur was a thin, horizontal disc, a spinning, not a vibration up and down. The noise it made, growing now into a whining roar, was like no sound of life that Chup had ever heard. The thing came rushing, almost falling, down toward the garden.

Chup pushed himself away from the wall. He had seen something of the magic that the Old World had called technology (though never a machine that flew), and knew the hopelessness of fighting with a sword against machines. He moved toward the doorway beside Charmian's empty divan; the flying thing looked too big to get in there. But before Chup reached the door, the wizard Hann was coming out to meet him, not as a foe but welcoming, with a flushed maidservant skipping beside him awkwardly, trying to finish tying a bandage on Hann's arm.

"The Lady Charmian sends you greetings . . . " Then Hann noticed the flying machine's approach, and Chup's attention to it. "No, no, Lord Chup, do not concern yourself; it is not a fighting device. Put up your sword. Come in! The Lady Charmian greets you, as I said, and expresses her apologies for all of this unfortunate . . . she will soon receive you. You have the golden charm with you, I trust? She begs you, let her maidens tend you now. When you are rested and refreshed . . ."

Chup was not really listening as he went on with Hann inside the door. Anyway the machine was not coming to Chup. Instead it descended close beside the corpse of Tarlenot. Just above the ground, the flyer hovered, while the shining whirl of speed on top roared down a blast of air that pressed down bushes, kicked up dust, and rippled grass. Along the headless metal body there stood symbols, meaningless to Chup:

VALKYRIE MARK V
718TH FIELD HOSPITAL BATTALION

In another moment the rounded metal body opened six secret holes, three on a side, and from them came extending hidden legs, sliding jointed things like insects' feelers grown monstrously large. These reached for Tarlenot and probed him, one delicate leg-tip clinging to the dull metal collar beside the great leaking leer of his wound. Then suddenly and effortlessly the flying thing gathered up Tarlenot's dead weight with its slender legs, drew it up and swallowed it into a coffin-sized cavity that gaped suddenly in the metal belly and as suddenly closed again. The six legs retracted and the Old World thing shot upward once again, roaring a louder noise and blasting the garden with a greater rush of air. It raced up toward the place whence it had come. Turned insect-sized again, it vanished into one of the windows where, according to Jarmer, the Beast-Lord Draffut dwelt.

Chup had stepped outside again, and remained

gaping upward until prompted by Hann's diplomatic voice. "When you have rested and refreshed yourself, Lord Chup, and dressed in finer garments, your lady waits to see you."

Lowering his eyes, Chup saw six serving girls approaching. All were young but ugly; his lady preferred her servants so, he knew, to heighten by contrast her own beauty. Carrying towels and garments and what might be jars of ointment, the girls advanced very slowly, looking almost too frightened to put one foot before another. Chup nodded. He would have to relax his guard sometime. "I would put down this sword that I have won, but I seem to have no scabbard."

Hann hastened to amend this lack, unburdening his own waist, wincing when he moved his wounded arm. "Here, take all. Indeed I think I am well rid of it. Let the shoemaker stick to his last."

When he had wiped and sheathed his sword, Chup let the servants of Charmian lead him along a short path into another garden, and from that into another wing of the same low, sprawling building that Charmian had entered. He could not yet see its full extent; perhaps all of Som's court lived in its separate apartments. In a luxurious room the servants stripped away Chup's filthy rags, and tended the light cut along his side with what seemed ordinary ointments, not the demon's cure. The girls' fear of him abated rapidly, and by the time they had immersed him in hot water in a sunken marble tub, they were talking almost freely back and forth among themselves. After serving Charmian, he thought, any other master must be a relaxation and a pleasure.

He hung the love-charm of springy golden hair upon the twisty hilt of his captured sword, and set both close beside him as he soaked and washed and soaked again. He was too weary to give the least thought to his attendants as females. Amid their nervous chatter, though, he caught their names:

Portia, with the blackest skin and hair that he had ever seen, and a bad scar on her face; Kath, blond and buxom, with eyes that looked in different ways; Lisa, shortest and youngest, nothing quite right about her looks; Lucia, shaped well enough except for her huge mouth and teeth; Samantha and Karen, looking like sisters or even twins, with sallow skins, pimples, and stringy hair bound up in the same peasant style as that of the other girls.

When Portia and Kath had finished scrubbing his back, Lisa and Lucia poured on rinse water, and Samantha and Karen held a towel.

When he had been clothed in rich garments, Karen and Lucia fed him soup and meat and wine. Between mouthfuls he touched the golden charm, safe now in an inner pocket of his tunic of soft black. He only tasted the wine, for already sleep hung like weighty armor on his eyelids. "Where is my Lady?" he demanded. "Is she coming here, or must I go to her?"

There was a moment's hesitation before Kath, with noticeable reluctance, answered: "If my Lord permits, I will go and see if she is ready to receive you." At this the other girls relaxed perceptibly.

His weariness was great, and he reclined on a soft couch. Though he had much to think about, his eyes kept closing of themselves. "Keep talking," he ordered the five girls. "You there, do you sing?" And Lisa sang, and Karen fetched out an instrument with strings. The music that they made was soft.

"You sing quite well and easily," Chup said, "for one who serves the Lady Charmian. How long have you been her servant?"

The girl paused in her song. "For half a year, my Lord, since I was brought to the Black Mountains."

"And what were you before?"

She hesitated. "I do not know. Forgive me, Lord, my head was hurt, my memory is gone."

"Sing on."

And then he was waking, with a start, the golden

charm clenched in his hand inside his pocket. It seemed that no long time had passed, for the sun still shone outside, and the young girls still made their soft music.

His tiredness was like the hands of enemies gripping all his limbs, but he could not rest until he had made sure of her, at the very least seen her once again. He arose and walked out of the building, into the garden under the upper mountain's looming bulk. On legs that pained but could not rest, he paced the paths and lawns, emptied now of men and cleaned of signs of violence. He entered the building where she had gone in. In a narrow passage he caught a whiff of perfume that woke old memories clamoring, and at a little distance heard Charmian's well-remembered laugh. He put aside a drapery.

Some distance inside a vast and elegantly female room, Charmian sat on an elaborate couch. She was facing Chup expectantly, though his coming had been soundless. The man who sat there with her, facing her, had fair hair that fell with a slight curl around his ears. His long, strong arms emerged from the short sleeves of a lounging suit of black and pink. As this man arose, turning toward Chup the wary, pouting eyes of Tarlenot, Chup could do nothing but stand frozen in the doorway, marking well the scar, wide and long but neatly healed, that ran down from the joining of neck and shoulder to vanish on the hairy chest—ran down from just below the metal collar that bore a little shiny spot left by a sword.

IV

Djinn of Technology

———————◆◆◆———————

The army of the West lay camped for the night, a day's march to the northeast of the Castle. Around them the plain was no longer a true desert, but a gentle sea of sparse grass, now drying and dying before the approaching winter. Once long ago the flocks of peacetime had grazed here.

Thomas now had with him more than four thousand soldiers, all holding in common a hard hatred of the East. The ranks of his own fighters of the Broken Lands had been greatly swollen by volunteers from Mewick's country and others in the south, from the offshore islands, and from the north, whence came warriors who wrapped themselves in unknown furs and made strange music from the horns of unknown beasts.

In the early evening the camp murmured with the feeding of the army and the digging of temporary defenses for the night, with the hundred matters of organization and repair that must be tended to before the second day's march. Inside Thomas's big tent were crowded the score of leaders he had called into a meeting.

The first matter that Thomas raised with them was the golden charm, and its sudden departure to the East. That the charm was magic of great power was obvious to all, and none blamed Rolf for having fallen so deeply under its influence that he had not spoken of it during the long months since he had found it, while it forced him to cherish secret thoughts of a woman he would otherwise have hated. Still he was downcast and somewhat ashamed as he sat at one side of the circle in the tent. Thomas, Gray, and a few others were at one end of the long test, their chairs around three sides of a plain table, the fourth side being open to the wide circle of onlookers who made themselves comfortable upon the matting of the floor. Thomas sat at the center of the table looking up at Gray who was on his feet and holding forth.

"Some of you know, but some do not," Gray was saying, "that I and other wizards of the West have for some years spent most of our time in a desperate search for the life of Zapranoth, the Demon-Lord in the Black Mountains."

There was a faint murmur round the tent. Rolf felt a little better, seeing how many of the others' faces mirrored his own ignorance of what the higher wizards did.

"It now seems possible," continued Gray, "that I stood next to the life of Zapranoth where I had scarcely thought to look for it: inside the walls of that strong Castle we left yesterday. It is possible—I think not likely—that the Demon-Lord's life was hidden in that twist of hair."

Eyes turned to Rolf, enough of them so that he felt he had to speak. "I had no thought or feeling of any demon near me, before or after the charm was taken from me."

Gray had paused to survey his audience. Now he said: "A number of you are still looking at me blankly, or frowning suspiciously at that young man. I am convinced that a short lecture on the ways of demons is in order." Having received a nod of agreement from Thomas, he went on. "The ordinary layman, soldier or not, has little hard knowledge of magic, though it almost daily influences his life. And to him the ways of demons are as unaccountable as those of earthquakes.

"I must make sure you understand me when I speak of our search for the life of Zapranoth. Now that we are on the march and can hope that spies have been left behind us, I can speak somewhat more freely. If you understand it may be that you can help, and if you help we may still succeed, and if we succeed in slaying the Demon-Lord of the Black Mountains it will count for more than would grinding the walls of Som's citadel to powder. Depend on that.

"Now. When I speak of finding a demon's life, I do not mean his active presence but his essence, secret and vulnerable—what the Old World seems to have called the soul. A demon's soul is separable in space from his personality. It is invisible, impalpable, and of vital importance, for only through it can he be destroyed. To keep his soul safe, he may hide it in any innocent thing: a flower, a tree, a human's hair, a rock, the foam of the sea, a spiderweb. He may keep it far away from him, where his enemies will not think to look for it, or near at hand where he will more easily know when it is threatened, and take steps in its defense. What is it?"

One of the fur-garbed Northmen got to his feet. "Is not Som the Dead the viceroy of the East, in the Black Mountains? And the Demon-Lord only his subordinate? Well, then. It would seem to me Zapranoth's life must be in Som's control."

Gray shook his head. "We think not. Those who rule the Empire of the East would not care to give any underling as much power as Som would have if Zapranoth were absolutely at his mercy. Therefore they have given Som only a lesser power of punishment over the Demon-Lord; so the two of them are constrained to eye each other jealously. It is a common pattern in the organization of the East."

Thomas and other senior leaders nodded. The man from the north sat down, and one from the south, from Mewick's country, asked: "If you wizards are baffled, trying to get at Zapranoth, how are we supposed to help?"

"How? First, understand the great importance of

our search. Then, if our campaigning takes you among strangers, friendly or neutral-seeming, say nothing of this matter, but listen carefully for any hint that there is information to be had. We will pay for it. We make no broadcast offers of reward, or half the fools and swindlers in the world would come to clog our path and waste our time, with spies and agents of the East among them. The chance that you will hear any clue is doubtless very small; but we must take every chance that we can get. Our search is desperate."

Gray took his seat, and Thomas rose. "Any more questions on our magic? Then let's go on to something else." He looked round as if gauging the temper of his hearers before continuing. "Though we are a real army now, it will be plain to all of you that our numbers are insufficient to storm any citadel as strong as Som's. You must know also that I have sent far afield, to every source of Western strength we are aware of, looking for help. You have been asking yourselves, and me, who may be sending troops to help us and where we are to meet them. The answer is: no troops are coming, or very few. We go on this campaign with no more men than we have now. Yet we are attacking the Black Mountains."

Thomas paused there, with every eye fixed on him intently. There was no murmur in the tent, but rather a deep hush; somewhere in the camp outside a blacksmith was shouting coarse imprecations at an animal.

He went on. "After, we make a feint to the north and perhaps a few skirmishes there with Som's outlying garrisons. In the Black Mountains is his power rooted, and only there can it be destroyed."

Someone urged: "Wait for the spring, then, for the birds' help! We cannot scale Som's cliffs against him. The birds could lift rope ladders for us, scout, bear messages, drop rocks upon the enemy, and use their talons, too!"

Thomas shook his head inflexibly and the murmur of approval that had started up died down. "We thought once that the Silent People might have stayed; we would have tried to warm them through the winter; but it is written in their bone-marrow, it seems, that they must fly south each autumn. There was nothing we or they could do about it. However, if the birds of the West will be absent from this campaign, at least the reptiles of the East will be sluggish and thick-blooded. And it is all very well to say, wait for spring, for the Silent People to fly north again. But so might Som be stronger then. And what of this human army we have gathered here and now? Shall we sit on our tails for another half year, hoping for improvement in our luck?"

That got something of the response Thomas must have hoped for. Folding his arms before him once again, he went on in a milder voice. "As for getting at Som in his citadel, we think that we have found a way. Gray?"

Once more the wizard arose, and spoke. As the plan he was proposing became clear, they cast looks at one another across the circle, with slowly lengthening faces. When the wizard paused, there were no questions. Probably, Rolf thought, because the only ones that came to mind were bluntly insulting about Gray's sincerity or sanity.

"As I said before, we are now on the march, away from prying eyes. Now the time has come to test what I propose, and if the test succeeds, to practice it. It will not be a usable technique till it is given considerable practice."

The stunned silence continued. Thomas dismissed the meeting, and while the others were filing out, called Rolf to one side where he stood with Gray. "Rolf. You have more experience with technology than anyone else we know of in our army. Gray will need an assistant in the project he just spoke of. I think you could do a good job of helping him."

Rolf grunted. "I don't know much, really."

"You have a knack." Thomas clapped both their shoulders, and said to Gray: "Take him, if you will, as your helper for the first experiment." Then Thomas turned quickly away, answering voices that were already calling him to see about some other business.

Gray and Rolf were left confronting each other in what was apparently a mutual lack of confidence. "Tell me, young one," the tall wizard said at last. "what do you know about the djinn?"

"Much like demons, are they not?"

Gray's gaze grew harder. "May you never be called upon to suffer in proportion to your ignorance of the world! Djinn are no more like demons than men are like the talking reptiles."

Continuing to talk Gray led Rolf from the tent. "Demons are, without exception, of the East. But the djinn are rather like elementals, neither good nor evil in themselves, and a human may call on them without being corrupted or consumed thereby."

"I see." Rolf nodded, not seeing much. "But what has this to do with technology, and the scheme you were proposing?" They were walking now through the uneven rows of tents, Gray heading for the out-skirts of the camp.

"Just this. The djinn I plan to call upon for help is unique, so far as I know, among his kind. He is a technologist, a builder and designer, I think superior in those fields to any human who has lived since the Old World. Now help me with some prep-arations, if you will."

It seemed to Rolf that he had little choice. Be-sides, the djinn as Gray described him was certainly intriguing.

They had got past the tents now, to a place near the camp's edge, not far from the latrines. It was a clear, open area perhaps fifty meters across, badly illuminated by a couple of torches on poles stuck in the ground. Rolf had earlier heard casual speculation that the place was being kept reserved for some magical purpose. Near its center was tethered a sullen-looking loadbeast wearing panniers that were bulky but did not seem heavy. From these Rolf and the wizard gathered bags and parcels which Gray opened on the sand. From them in turn he took small objects which, Rolf again helping as directed, he set out on the ground in a regular and careful pattern. The things looked to Rolf for the most part like toys for some carpenter's child: there were miniature hammers, wooden wheels, a tiny saw, small brace and bit, and other little tools.

"Rolf, once you rode upon an Old World vehicle that moved across the land without a beast to pull it; you learned its secrets of control, and rode it into battle."

"That is so." Rolf had finished laying out his portion of the pattern.

"Had you ever any indication that it might fly?"

"No, Gray." His answer was emphatic. "It was of metal, and heavier than a big house, and it had no sign of wings."

Gray shrugged. "Well, certainly they had many machines that did not fly; but they had some that did. And some of them still do, I think, though that does not concern us at this moment. What I proposed in meeting just now was not as mad as some thought. Machines can fly, and I intend that we shall use them to assault the cliffs of the Black Mountains." Squinting at the arrangement of toy tools on the ground, Gray grunted with satisfaction, and began to draw with his staff (it occurred to Rolf that he had not noticed any staff in Gray's hands until just now) a diagram of straight lines surrounding the symbolic tools. "The djinn that I will summon up will build for us a vehicle which we will then operate ourselves. I think its pilotage will not be too difficult, for intelligent men who have a little nerve and imagination."

Gray stood his staff beside him on the ground;

there it remained, as if it had taken root. He rummaged in the beast's panniers again, and produced a paper that he unrolled and showed to Rolf.

"I have made this sketch from drawings left by the ancients of some of their simpler flying machines. Other types they made as well, that were heavier than air, and winged like birds, but the technology of those remains somewhat beyond my grasp; and what I cannot understand, I cannot order the djinn to build. However, the type that I have shown here should suit us well."

Rolf studied the sketch. It showed, apparently in midair, a rimmed platform or shallow basket, supported at each of its four corners by a cluster of lines, the lines in turn reaching tautly upward to four great globes above. A mast rose from the center of the platform; small sails bellied, and pennants fluttered, showing the direction of the breeze. Inside the basket, four men rode.

"These globes from which the flying craft depended were made of some elastic fabric" Gray explained. "Sometimes filling them with hot air was enough to make them rise."

Rolf considered silently. *Was* Gray mad? But wait—hot air did rush up the chimney.

"But with the djinn to labor for us, we shall do far better. Our globes will be made of thin metal, much stronger and safer, and in them there will be nothing."

"Nothing?" Rolf tried to make the question sound intelligent.

Gray studied him, and sighed. Perhaps he wondered if he should request a more intelligent aide. "Consider: Why does a ship, or any chunk of wood, float on the water?"

"Because—because it is lighter than water. Too light to sink."

"Ah. Very true." Gray smiled, and tapped the paper with his finger. "Now, when all the air has been exhausted from these metal spheres—experiments have already shown me that air indeed has weight—when the weight of this whole apparatus is thus made less than the weight of an equal volume of air, what will this flying craft do?"

"It will weigh less than air?" Yes, it all sounded mad; but Rolf despite himself felt some enthusiasm growing for this mad scheme. Wild as Gray's ideas were, they somehow began to feel right in Rolf's mind.

Gray spoke more rapidly, pleased that someone could halfway understand him. "Air is very light, true. But nothingness is lighter still. I tell you, the ancients made the idea work. Are you ready to try it with me, young technologist? I will need quick hands to help me and a quick mind, too, perhaps; Thomas tells me you have both, and I believe him. Of course you will help, you are ordered to. But are you really *with* me in this enterprise?"

Rolf took the time to give the question honest thought. "I am."

Gray nodded. With a flourish, then, he beckoned to his balancing staff—that sprang lightly through the air into his hand. "Be silent for a moment now, while I evoke the djinn. He is an odd creature, even of his kind, irascible and not well-meaning. But he must labor for us, though he cares nothing for East or West, or for any man or demon."

The calling-up was accomplished with quick confidence. After making a few controlled gestures over the array of toy tools and drawn lines, Gray uttered in a low rapid voice words that Rolf could not quite hear. Fire appeared in the air before the wizard, with a belching of soot and acrid smoke, and accompanied by a sound of rapid pounding, as by unseen, crude and heavy implements. The voice of the djinn rolled forth, sounding one moment like splintering wood, the next like clashing metal. "I come as bidden, master. What is your command?"

Gray unrolled his sketch and held it forth toward the flaming image of the djinn, meanwhile intoning:

"I first let be created four such great hollow spheres such as you see represented here—"

The djinn's voice hammered, interrupting. "You *let* be? That means you do not hinder?"

Asperity was in Gray's voice. "It means that I command! I order you to do it, and be quick! The specifications for the globes are as follows . . ."

The djinn did not dispute him further, but maintained its sooty glow in silence, evidently listening. A moment after Gray had finished detailing his order, there appeared from nowhere four crude blocks of metal, each half as big as a man. In another moment the blocks were glowing hot. At once there arose a mighty screeching, and a banging as of invisible hammers.

The few soldiers who had been standing in the middle distance, watching, were being joined momentarily by ever-growing numbers of their fellows, drawn by the prospect of seeing something spectacularly unusual in the way of magic. The camp had doubtless heard by now several versions of what had happened at the meeting in Thomas's tent. Rolf, for his part, backed up a few paces, and considered putting his fingers in his ears to dull the noise. The blocks of metal glowed incandescent and expanded under the powerful working of the djinn. They stretched out and up into enormous sheets of fiery metal, which then began to curve themselves, perfectly and surely, into spheres.

When the spheres, each the size of a small house, were almost completely closed, the djinn left them to cool on the sand. Meanwhile he received from Gray the specifications for the platform of the flying device, and for the ropes and sails and their attachments.

"So I let it be done!" Gray concluded.

The djinn began to work again, extruding from its smoke long coils of twine. And as it worked, it grumbled. "Just so you understand that it is I am gathering all the stuffs and doing all the work that you are letting. It does not come from nothingness, you know.''

"Nothingness," said Gray sharply, "is what I want inside the spheres—when the craft is finished, we are aboard, and all's in readiness for flight. Then will I give you the order to empty them and seal them.''

The djinn emitted a burst of noise somewhat like the working of a broken sawmill. It took Rolf a little time to understand that this was laughter. "Nothingness! You do not know what you are ordering—beg pardon, what you are letting, master.''

"Contrary dolt!" A vein now stood upon Gray's forehead. Rolf made a prudent mental note that the wizard was not notably long on patience. Gray went on: "By nothingness I mean a lack of air, a vacuum, nullity; such as you yourself will soon become if you irritate me too sorely!''

The djinn evidently did not regard the threat as idle, for the work did pick up speed, and for the time being at least there were no further grumblings. What seemed to be a multitude of invisible hands spun twine into stout ropes, and fastened ropes to the basket as it was fabricated. It was of a size to hold three or four people without crowding, with a waist-high rim all round, woven of tough, flexible withes, and seemingly very light. Each corner of the square basket was secured with several ropes to one of the great metal spheres. Their overshadowing bulks creaked as they cooled, and all but hid the basket from observation. At Gray's direction, a central mast was now stepped in, and sails and pennants made and stowed folded in the bottom of the basket. Water and provisions, from more commonplace sources, went in also.

Full night had come when Gray was satisfied that all was in readiness for flight. He himself was the first to step into the basket, with a somewhat cautious scissoring of his long legs. "Now master Rolf, if you will." And Rolf, feeling almost evenly balanced between eagerness and reluctance, hopped nimbly aboard.

Thomas and several others had drawn near, to wish the voyagers well and to observe at close range whatever might happen next. When the last word of encouragement had been called in between the surrounding metal globes, Gray gestured for silence. Facing the smoky glow of the djinn's image, he swept his pointing hand to one after another of the four spheres as he cried out: "Now, let there be exhausted from them all the air and other vapors, and let them then be sealed shut!"

A quartet of hissing noises suddenly surrounded the basket, issuing from the four orifices left in the spheres. Rolf felt his hair stirred by one of the jets of air. Tensely he gripped the basket's railing, waiting for the first surge of flight.

And almost at once the four enormous globes did stir themselves. But not to rise. Instead, as their hissings began to be drowned out by ringings and portentous metal groans, they rolled from side to side on the sand, they lurched and crumpled and deformed themselves. The sphere in front of Rolf seemed to be struck by some giant and invisible mace; it sounded a deafening clang as it drew into itself a vast dent that bent its surface to its center. Then all four spheres, in a great blacksmith's uproar of tortured metal, were shrivelling and flattening like so many fruit-husks thrown into a fire. As their obscuring bulks shrank down, Rolf saw Thomas and others tumbling away with as little thought of dignity or face as they would have shown before an enemy ambush that caught them unarmed. Rolf had one leg over the basket rim again, and would have fled himself, but one direction looked as perilous as another. Meanwhile the basket stayed firmly seated on the sand, only swaying with Gray's vociferous anger. The wizard spouted words at a tremendous rate, while Rolf dodged this way and that to avoid his gesturing arms.

Silence returned as suddenly as it had fled. The
metal spheres, now reduced to shrunken, twisted
wads of scrap, were still. Gray's speech faltered and
ran down, and for the moment silence was complete. There quickly ensued a murmur of laughter
from part of the watching army, a murmur that dis-
solved before it could grow too large, when Gray
swept his glare around him like a weapon. The dim
masses of people beyond the torchlight began to
scatter and drift off; a number of them, once they
had got some distance away, seemed compelled to
utter muted whooping noises.

Thomas and others, drawing near once more,
spitting dust and brushing it from their clothes, did
not seem much amused. But none of them dared yet
say anything to Gray.

Gray drew in a big breath, and shouted one more
outburst at the djinn. Its flaming, fuming scroll
flared on apparently unperturbed.

"Oh great master," it answered in its clattering
voice, "such a curse as you have just delivered
would pain me like the grip of Zapranoth — if I were
in fact such a disobedient traitor as you say I am.
But, as things are, I feel no ill effects. I have followed
your instructions to the letter."

"Ahhg! Technology!" Gray flung down his arms.
He climbed out of the basket, in his excitement of
disgust catching his foot on the rim and nearly falling. Lowering his voice, he said to those nearby: "It
speaks the truth. Technology! How can any man
who means to keep his sanity go far in such an art?"

Rolf, having got out of the basket too, was thinking. Hesitantly he asked: "Can I put questions to this
djinn?"

"Why not?" Gray snapped, as if answering only
with the easiest thing to say.

Rolf turned to address the fiery image. "You,
there. What made the balls crumple up like that?"

There was a brief silence, as if the djinn were

assessing its new questioner. Then with a clatter the answer came: "Little master, they crumpled because the air was taken out of them."

"Why?"

"Why not? The outside air pushed in with all its weight, and there was only thin metal to resist it."

Gray had spoken of his experiments, showing that air had weight. The wizard looked uncomfortable, but with a sharp motion of his head he signed Rolf to go on with his questioning.

Rolf considered. It seemed to him that Gray's theory was basically correct: a machine made lighter than air should rise in air, as wood rose in water; and air most certainly had weight. But obviously there were traps and dangers awaiting the technologist.

Rolf asked Gray: "Must it speak the truth to us?"

"Yes." Gray sighed. "But not the whole truth; that's the catch. Go on, go on, ask it more. Perhaps you have a better head for this than I."

Rolf took thought, tried to put from his mind the fact that everyone present was watching and listening to him, and faced the djinn again. "Suppose you make the walls of the globes thicker and stronger. That should keep them from being crushed when you take out the air."

"You are right," said the djinn immediately. "Shall I rebuild them so?"

"And would they still be light enough, when emptied, to lift us and the basket with them?"

There was a short delay. "No." This time Rolf thought he detected disappointment.

He folded his arms, and took a few short paces to and fro. "Tell me, djinn, what did the folk of the Old World do when they wished to fly?"

"They made a flying machine, and rode in it. I myself was born with the New World, of course, and never saw them. But so I have been told, and so I truly believe."

"How did they make these flying machines?"

"Describe a way, and I will tell you if it is right or wrong."

Rolf looked at Gray, who shook his head and told him: "I cannot compel it to greater helpfulness. The djinn must give us what it knows of the truth, in answer to our questions, but if it wishes to be grudging it can yield only a small fragment at a time."

Rolf nodded, accepting the rules of the game, which he found more and more fascinating. "Djinn. Were these flying devices lighter than the air?"

"Some of them."

"Had they lifting spheres, as big as these were?"

"Sometimes."

"Yet their spheres were not crushed."

"That is true."

The audience was silent. The time of half a dozen breaths had passed before Rolf chose his next question. "Were their lifting spheres empty?"

"No." The monosyllable had a forced, reluctant sound.

"They were filled, then, with something lighter than the air?"

"They were."

It was midnight before Rolf had extracted from the djinn what seemed to be the last necessary bit of information, and Gray could issue new orders: " — that the new spheres be made of fabric such as you have described, airtight and capable of stretching; and that they be filled, by this lighter-than-air gas that will not burn, to the point where they will lift the basket with us in it."

Shortly before dawn, having managed a few hours' sleep in the meantime, Gray and Rolf were once more in the basket, attended by an audience much smaller and less hopeful-looking than that of the previous evening. Once more Gray gave orders to the djinn. The new balloons, that had replaced the crumpled metal spheres, rose from the sands as they inflated, then tugged boldly at their strong tethers, pulling them taut. The basket creaked and moved, and Rolf beheld the desert floor go dropping silently from beneath his feet.

The few who watched the launching cheered and waved. The camp was already astir with preparations for the day's march, and now a wider cheer went up to greet the swift-ascending flyer. Looking down upon an earth much darker than the lightening sky, Rolf saw his comrades' breakfast fires shrink steadily. The airborne flying machine was drifting slowly but steadily to the north. Gray was issuing sharp orders, planned beforehand, to the djinn, whose smoky image drifted without weight or apparent effort beside the basket. There came a hiss as flying gas was vented from the bags. Their giant shapes were spheres no longer but pressed together above the mast by their own bulging.

The hissing continued, as Gray had ordered, until their ascent had been stopped, or so the djinn informed them. Rolf could not say from one moment to the next that they were really on the same level, and he would have been hard put to judge exactly how high they were. The fires of the camp were now a scattering of sparks at some distance to the south, and the last people Rolf had seen there had been shrunken to the stature of small insects. Not that he was worried about their height. The tight grip he had taken on the rim of the basket when it lifted, was now loosening. Enjoyment was winning out steadily over fright.

Gray, too, seemed pleased. After exchanging with Rolf opinions that all was going well, he resumed giving orders to the djinn, for the attachment of rigging to the mast, and the readying of sails.

The wizard called out jovially: "Rolf, have you ever steered a sailing ship?"

"No. Though I have lived my whole life near enough to the sea."

"It matters not, I have experience. Once we get up a sail, I'll show you how to tack against the wind.

We'd best not fly by daylight, there may be reptiles scouting."

Things did not immediately go right with the rigging. Rolf was called upon to hold lines, tie knots, and pull. A sail soon rose upon the mast, but then hung in utter limpness. Gray, scowling again, hauled this way and that on lines and cloth, but the sail would not so much as flutter. He hoisted a pennant, but it too drooped like chain mail. Clenching his fists, Gray muttered: "Is this some countering magic? I sense none. Yet there was a breeze before we lifted from the ground."

"There is one yet," said Rolf, nodding to the ever-shrinking pattern of the camp's cookfires, dimming now with the approach of dawn. "Or what is carrying us northward?" But he could not feel a breath of moving air upon his face.

Gray took one look back at the camp, and called the djinn to question. "Why does the wind not belly out my sail?"

"Name a reason, and I will say if it be true." The clatter of the djinn's voice became something like a cackle.

Gray sputtered.

Rolf asked: "Djinn. Are we becalmed because our whole craft is already moving with the wind, like part of it? Instead of the wind pushing past us?"

"It is so."

Angrily Gray flared up. "There were sails drawn in the Old World pictures—" Then a thought struck him silent; after a moment he grumbled: "Of course, those drawings may have been sheer fancy; they did that sometimes. But they *did* have real airships. How then did they steer them? Rolf, question it some more. And I will think, meanwhile."

Rolf tried not to think of how fast they might be drifting, and how high. "Djinn, tell me. Did the ancients ever use sails?"

Clatter, cackle. "Not to fly."

"Did they use paddles to propel their airships?"

"Never."

"Rudders to steer them?"

There was a reluctant-seeming pause. "Yes."

"Yes?" Rolf pounced without a second thought. "Then fetch us such a rudder, here, at once!"

The air around them seemed to sigh, as with a giant's effort, or perhaps the satisfaction of a djinn. Then arrived the rudder, here and at once indeed; it was a wall of metal, curving, monstrous, overgrown, wedged between balloon and basket so that it bent the mast and stretched the ropes and all but crushed the occupants. Shaped roughly like a door for some great archway, the rudder was a good twelve meters long. Its longest, straightest edge, turned downward now, was nearly a meter thick; coming out of the flatness of this edge were festoons of cabling and the ends of metal pipes.

The balloon sank horrendously under the huge load. Gray, bent double under the slab whose main weight was fortunately carried by the basket's rim, cried out an order. In an instant the great mass was gone. The airship leaped up again, Gray stood, and Rolf recovered himself from the position into which he had been forced, almost entirely out of the basket.

There was silence for a little while, except for gasps and wheezings. When Gray spoke at last, his voice was icily detached. "In magic, hasty words are ill-advised. So I learned long ago."

"I will not utter any more of them. Believe me."

"Well. I have blundered too, this night. Let us learn from our mistakes and then forget them, if we can."

"Gray, may I ask the djinn a cautious question?"

"Ask him what you will. Our troubles seem to stem from giving him orders."

Turning to the unperturbed scroll of smoke, Rolf asked: "Did the Old Worlders ever use such a rudder as you brought to us to steer a flying craft like this one, lighter than the air and with no means of making headway through the air?'' He was imagining himself in a boat, drifting with a current; and he saw clearly in his mind that the rudder in the boat was useless, for there was no streaming of water around it.

''No.'' The monosyllabic answer seemed all innocence.

Gray asked: ''Did they ever steer craft like this at all?''

''No.''

The two humans exchanged a weary look. Gray said: ''I had better give orders for the gradual deflation of the bags, so that we drift no farther. It will take our men a while to reach us as it is.''

''I see no danger in that order,'' Rolf approved cautiously. As gas began to hiss from the bags again, he turned to the east, where now the sun lanced at him from above the distant range of black. There was one peak that seemed to tower above the rest, its head lost in a wreath of cloud that looked much higher still than the balloon.

Gray seemed to know where he was looking. ''There lies the citadel of Som the Dead. On those cliffs—can you see them?—that rise up halfway on the highest mount. There's where we must somehow land part of our army.''

And somewhere there, thought Rolf, my sister may be still alive. ''We will find a way,'' he said. With his hand he struck the basket rim. ''We will make this work.''

''Here comes the ground,'' said Gray.

The landing was a tumble, but it broke no bones.

V

Som's Hoard

———◆■◆———

Chup stood frozen in the doorway, watching as the man whom he had killed stood up, fresh and healthy as when their duel had started. Tarlenot, starlted by Chup's entrance, turned and got up quickly. But when he saw Chup's paralysis of astonishment, he relaxed enough to offer him a slight bow and a mocking smile.

Charmian, who had looked up as if expecting Chup, said calmly: "Leave us now, good Tarlenot."

Tarlenot, with the air of one who had completed his visit anyway, bowed once more, this time to her. "I shall. As you know, I must soon give up this happy collar for a while, and take to the road again. Of course I mean to see you again before I set out—"

She waved him off. "If not, you shall when you return. Go now."

He frowned briefly at her, decided not to argue, and gave Chup one more look of amusement. Then Tarlenot withdrew, going out through a doorway at the long chamber's other end.

Charmian now turned herself completely toward Chup, and at the sight of him began to giggle. In a moment she was rolling over on her couch, quite gracefully, in her mirth. And she laughed with a loud clear peal, like some innocent teasing girl.

Chup moved unsteadily toward her. Still looking after Tarlenot, he said: "My blade went this far down in him. This far. I saw him die."

She still laughed merrily. "My hero, Chup! But

you are so astonished. It is worth all the vexation, just to see you so."

For his part, Chup was very far from laughter. "What powers of sorcery do you have here? What do battles mean, and warriors' lives, when dead men jump up grinning?"

Her mirth quieted. She began to eye Chup as if with sympathy. "It was not sorcery, dear Chup, but his Guardsman's collar that saved him."

"No collar stopped my blade, I cut down to his heart. I know death when I see it."

"Dear fool! I did not mean that at all. Of course you cut him down. He died. You beat and killed him, as I knew you would. But then he was restored by the Lord Draffut."

"There is no way of restoring . . . " Chup's voice trailed off.

She nodded, following his thought. "Yes my Lord. As it was done for you, by the fluid of the Lake of Life. Since you do not wear the collar of Som's Guard, I had to risk the Beast-Lord's great displeasure by having the fluid stolen for you—by one of the demons he so hates. But I would face greater risks than that, to have you with me." Her face and voice were innocent and proud. "Come, sit beside me here. Have you the little trinket with you, that was woven of my hair?"

He walked to the soft couch, and sat down beside his unclaimed bride. From his pocket he brought out the golden charm, clenched in his hand.

"No, keep it for me, my good Lord, until I tell you how it must be used. Keep it and guard it well. With no one else will it be so safe." Charmian took his hand, but only to press his fingers tighter around the knot of yellow hair.

He put the thing back in his pocket. Still foremost in his thought was the resurrection he had witnessed. "So, Tarlenot will be magically healed, whenever and however he is slain?"

"If he falls here, in sight of Som's citadel and with

his collar on. Did you not hear him say just now that he will leave his Guardsman's collar here when he goes out as a courier again? The valkyries will not fly more than a kilometer or two from the citadel."

"The what?"

"The valkyries, the flying machines of the Old World, that take the fallen Guardsmen up to Draffut to be healed. They get but little practice now."

"What is this Guard of Som's?"

"An elite corps of men he thinks reliable." She had released his hand and was talking in a businesslike way. "They number about five hundred; there are no more collars than that."

He observed: "You have not yet managed to get one of these protective collars for yourself."

"I will depend upon my strong Lord Chup for protection; we will see that you have a collar, of course, as soon as possible."

"You have been depending on the strong Lord Tarlenot till now, I gather. Well, I will wait and catch him with his collar off."

Charmian laughed again, this time even more delightedly, and curled up amid her silks. "That messenger? Why, you are joking, lord. You must know I am only using him, and to make him really useful I must lead him on. My only true thoughts are for you."

Grimly and thoughtfully, he said: "I remember that you do not have true thoughts."

Now she was hurt. Her eyes looked this way and that, then sought him piteously and fluttered. One who did not know her as he did might easily have been convinced. He knew her, and was not fooled; but she was still his bride, and all-important to him. He frowned, wondering why he did not wonder. There must be a reason, and he ought to have remembered it, but somehow it eluded him.

"My every thought has been for you," his all-important bride was pouting. "True, when you arrived today I pretended to be angry—surely you

could not have been deceived by that? I wanted
Tarlenot to fight you, so you would put him in his
place. You must have understood that! Could *he*
ever have beaten you, even on the sickest day you've
ever had?''

"Why, yes, he could, and handily."

She avoided his reaching hand and jumped to her
feet. "How can you dare to think that I have ever
meant you harm? If you will be rude enough to ask
for proof of my intentions, I can only point out that
here you are, restored to life and health and power.
And who is responsible for your restoration, if not
I?''

"Very well, you saved me. But for your own
reasons. You wanted this." Again he pulled the
charm out of his pocket. Looking down at the soft,
shiny thing resting so lightly in his open hand, he
could remember vaguely that he had felt misgivings
about picking it up for the first time, but he could
not remember why. He asked: "What do you want it
for?''

"Put it away, please." When he had done that,
Charmian sat down again and took his hand between hers. "I want to use it. To make you Viceroy in
the Black Mountains, in Som's place."

He grunted in surprise, beyond mere disbelief.

"Be at ease, my lord," she reassured him. "The
wizard Hann, who is with us in this enterprise, has
made this apartment proof against Som's spies."

"*I* came in quite unnoticed."

"Not by me. I wanted you to enter, my good lord."
Her small hands pressed his fingers tenderly. "Ah,
but it is good to have you sitting with me once again.
You will be Lord of High Lords here, with Zapranoth
and Draffut as your vassals and only the distant
Emperor himself above; and I will be your consort,
proud beside you."

He made another boorish noise.

Unruffled, she pressed his arm. "Chup, do you

doubt that I would like to be the lady of a viceroy?"

"I don't doubt that."

Her nails spurred his forearm. "And do you think that I would want some lesser man than you beside me, one who could not hold such a prize when we had won it, or try for something higher still. By all the demons, you underrate me if you do!"

Viceroy, Lord of High Lords . . . armies numbering tens of thousands under his command . . . beside him, Charmian, looking as she did now. He could no longer *wholly* doubt what she was saying. "Has Viceroy Som no need of you, to hold his place and help him try for something higher still?"

Her eyes flashed anger, mixed with determination. "I want a living man, not dead . . . but you are right, my lord, Som is the key. We must dispose of him." She said it easily. "He gave me shelter when my father fell, thinking I would be useful to him one day; I convinced him you would be useful too. He does not know that you have brought the means of his downfall."

Chup's manner was still scornful. "And what are we to do with Som the Dead? How shall we topple him?"

Her eyes, that had gone to feast upon some distant vision, came back to his unwaveringly. "The circlet woven of my hair must go into his private treasure hoard, unknown to him. Only thus can he be made vulnerable to—certain magic that we shall use against him."

"He must have protection against such charms."

"Of course. But Hann says that the one you carry is of unequalled power."

Chup said: "You speak much of this wizard Hann, and what he says. What does he gain, by helping you?"

Charmian pouted. "I see I must soothe down your pointless jealousy again. Hann wants only vengeance, for some punishment that Som inflicted on him long ago. I know that Hann gives no impression of great skill at magic, yet he is stronger in his way than Elslood was, or Zarf—''

"Then why can he not make a stronger charm than Elslood wrought?" He thought he could feel it in his pocket, like a circle of heavy fire.

She shook her head impatiently. "I do not understand it perfectly, but it seems that Elslood, wanting me to care for him, stole some of my hair and wove the charm. But he tapped some power greater than he understood, the charm only made him dote all the more on me. Never mind. We need not struggle with these technicalities of magic. All that you need worry about, my lord, is getting the charmed circlet woven of my hair into Som's private treasure hoard."

"How?"

"I have already gone far in learning ways and making plans for that. But the execution of the plan requires someone like yourself, my lord; and who is there but you?"

"How?" His voice was still heavy with his skepticism.

She seemed about to tell him, but first she recounted once more the joys of being viceroy. Her soft voice wore him down, so that he passed the midpoint between doubting and belief; all things were possible, when his bride whispered that they were.

Now she was telling him what he must do: "Now hear me, my lord. Three things must fall together ere we strike. First, the human guards who watch the outer entrance to the treasure vault must be those we have suborned. Second—are you listening?—the new breed of centipedes in the second room must not yet have hatched. Thirdly, the word for quieting the demons in the inner vault must be the one we know . . ."

Demons again. He ceased to listen. He was wearying quickly of all these endless words, even if they came from her, when she herself was here. Shaking his head to break the spell of words, he reached for her.

"My lord, wait. Hear me. This is vital—"

But he would not wait, nor hear her any longer, and with a small sigh of vexation she let him have his way.

On the next day, when he had truly rested, there came to him officers of Som's Guard, who wished to question Chup about the military situation in the West. Chup related the rumors common in the Broken Lands, for what they might be worth. He told the officers what he had observed of troop movements, from his beggar's post, and of other matters bearing on the military, the conditions of roads and livestock in the Broken Lands, the feelings and prosperity of the populace, the state of the harvest. He could give the Guardsmen little comfort, except as regarding the relative smallness of Thomas's force. Thomas would need great reinforcement before he could attempt an attack upon this citadel.

Chup was soon sitting at ease with the officers, military men like himself. He was now dressed like them in a uniform of black, except that he had as yet no rank, and of course no Guardsman's collar. In the course of exchanging soldiers' talk he asked about the collars. He could not imagine how it would feel to enter a fight with the knowledge that you could be glued together again if you were hacked apart; would it be a spur or a hindrance to the most effective action? Would a man who wearied let himself be killed to gain a rest?

One of the officers shook his head, and raised one finger. It ended in a tiny abnormal loop of flesh, instead of a fingernail. "The healing's not that safe or certain. Things sometimes go wrong, up in Lord Draffut's house. A man who's badly mangled going in may well come out too crooked to walk straight.

And those who've been too long lifeless when the
valkyries pick 'em up may never again be smarter
than little animals.''

The other officer nodded his scarred head. ''Still,''
he said, ''I think none of us are likely to turn in our
collars.''

''See much fighting here?'' Chup asked.

''Not since we came here, and Draffut handed out
his collars; he was here first, you know, before the
East or West . . . We do grow somewhat stale, those
of us who stay inside these mountains. Nothing but
a peasant uprising from time to time. But we practice. We'll handle this Thomas if he comes.''

Chup was invited to visit the officers' club on a
lower level of the citadel, where wine and gambling
and fresh peasant girls were available. He got up and
strolled with the two men to sample the wine; as for
the dice and the women, he had no money at the
moment, and could not imagine himself wanting
any woman but one.

Walking the main, buried corridors of the citadel,
Chup took note of the fighting men he saw. He supposed the garrison might number a thousand if
all were mobilized; but the five hundred elite
Guardsmen should be easily able to hold the natural defenses of the place against Thomas's four
thousand or so. A few of the Guardsmen were
grotesquely misshapen with old scars, of wounds
no man could ordinarily survive, though they were
active still; this confirmed what the officer had said
about the uncertainty of being healed.

Chup had other things to watch for on his walk to
the officers' club and back again, through rooms
and passages carved from the mountain's rock. In
one large chamber, decorated with some ancient
artisan's frieze of unknown men and creatures, he
spotted without paying it any obvious attention the
entrance to the passage that Charmian had told him
to watch for. It was an unmarked tunnel leading
downward and yet farther into the mountain. It was

this way that, by many turns and branches she had described, would lead him to Som's own treasure hoard.

Again and again during the next two days she repeated her instructions to him; by then he had ceased to doubt her word on anything at all. And then she awoke him in the night, to tell him that the time had come, the three requirements had fallen together. Tomorrow he must try to reach the treasure vault of Som.

He strode into the high, frieze-corniced room with the air of a man upon some important errand, as indeed he was. The room was an intersection of two corridors, and held people passing continually to and fro. No one paid attention as Chup turned aside into the downward way that led toward the treasure; it led to other things as well, and was not guarded here.

Chup walked unarmed with any blade or club; he must not kill today, must leave no traces of his passage. For weapons, he carried Charmian's knowledge of Som's secrets, gathered he knew not how, but trust her to manage that, in a world of men; and his own boldness, and speed of mind and body; and three words of magic; and a pocketful of dried fruit, innocent to the eye and taste. Hann had demonstrated that a human might eat of it without effect.

A few people passed Chup, coming toward him through the tunnel he descended. Then the way branched, once and again, and now there were no other walkers. The branch that Chup had been taught to follow was a narrow way, and it went on without another intersection for some distance. Now and then it broke out of its walls into a large cave, where it formed a suspended walkway across chasms whose depths were lost in darkness. Sunlight filtered down into the big caves through hidden openings somewhere high above. Along the

buried parts of the way, a few cheap lampstands
cast some illumination. There were no signs, nor
any evidence that any goal of much importance lay
in this direction.

So far, all was as Charmian had foretold. And now,
here, just as she had said, the path bridged a wider
crevasse than usual, and then branched once more.
The right way, she had told him, led up into the
viceroy's private quarters. The left side, narrower,
was the one that Chup must take.

Now at last there were posted warning signs.
Chup had no doubt of what they meant, though he
did not stop to try to puzzle out the letters. He also
ignored another, blunter, warning: a bundle of
mummied hands that were no doubt supposed to be
those of would-be trespassers hung like a cluster of
dried vegetables above the way. He moved his head
slightly as he walked beneath, not wanting the dead
fingers to brush his hair. His pulse went quicker. If
he were stopped and questioned now, it would be
hard to say convincingly that he had seen no warning.

A final abrupt turn, and Chup's path came to an
end against a massive, unmarked door. This too he
found as Charmian had described it: so strongly
built that a ram would be needed to break it down.
Having no sword hilt to rap out a signal with, Chup
put his knuckles to the job. The door resounded no
more than would a massive tree stump, but someone must have been listening for the little noise, for
it was answered quickly. A dim face peeked out at
Chup through a small grill. A sliding of bars and
rattle of chains, and the great door moved inward
just enough for him to enter.

He stepped into a barren, rock-walled chamber
about ten meters square. The two men in
Guardsmen's collars standing watch had been given
no chairs or other furniture to lure them into relaxation. Directly across from the door where Chup had
entered, a ladder five or six meters long stood lean-

ing against the wall; beside the ladder was the room's only visible aperture besides the door, a narrow hole that led down into darkness. Thick candles in wall sconces lit the guardroom adequately.

One of the men who greeted Chup was hardly more than half a man in size, his legs being grotesquely short. The other guard was of ordinary stature, and sound of limb, but his face was the strangest Chup had ever seen on living man, a wall of scars from which one live eye gleamed like something trapped. According to Charmian, these men had been enlisted in her cause by promises of better healing when she came to power. The two of them closed up and chained and barred the great door tight as soon as Chup was through it; and then they looked at Chup expectantly, but saying nothing.

He had wasted no time either, but had crossed the chamber to look down into the hole. He could see nothing in the darkness there. "Where's the beast?" he asked. "I mean, in which part of its room?"

The scarred man made a nervous sound. "Hard to say. You've got some means of putting it to sleep?"

"Of course. But I'd like to know just where to toss the bait."

They came and stood beside him at the hole, peering down and listening, muttering to each other, trying to locate the beast. They were nervous for his welfare. If his attempt miscarried down below, their complicity in it would be discovered when Chup — alive or dead — was found. It seemed a long time before the dwarfed man raised a hand for Chup's attention, and pointed to a quarter of the room below. Bending over the pit, straining his ears, Chup thought he could barely hear a dry patter that must be made by the beast's multitude of feet.

"There, there, yes," the scarred man whispered. "It'll be behind you as you go down the ladder."

They got ready for him the long ladder — Chup saw now that it was really an extremely slim and elegant stair, complete with handrail, fit for Som to use when he went down to count his gold—and now they slid the ladder down.

Chup went down facing the ladder, about one third of its length, before he tossed his first piece of dried fruit. He heard the hundred feet shiver before he saw the rail-thin, cat-quick body; he could not tell for sure whether the bait had been taken. Hann had said that two pieces swallowed should afford Chup time enough to complete his mission. He let his eyes become somewhat more accustomed to the gloom before he tossed a second bait, and he saw this one snapped up by the first pair of delicate legs, flicked up into the tiny, harmless mouth. A moment only passed before the beast shivered, twitched extravagantly, and began to curl its body. Its hundred legs in disarray, it slid down springily to the floor, showing Chup as it bent the hundred branching slivers of its whiplike tail.

Chup cautiously went down the rest of the ladder. The centipede remained completely quiet. He left the ladder and paced toward the door that led to the next lower level; and now the dryness of fear was growing in his throat. Behind him he heard the ladder being drawn up; so it had been planned, in case some officer should come while he was down below.

There was a bloated bulk of darkness that he only just avoided stepping on, when it made a feeble movement in his path. He had been told of this also. It had been a man, and was still alive, nourishing the larvae of the centipede inside itself. Perhaps its hands would someday join the thieves' bundle over the tunneled walk; perhaps it had in fact once been a would-be thief.

In the faint light from below he could make out the way to the next lower level: an ordinary doorway led to a simple solid stair of stone, narrow and curving but quite open. What was below had no desire nor occasion to come up, and the centipede would be too frightened to go down.

Chup went down, armed with the three words of

magic Hann had taught him. They weighed now like swallowed arrows in his throat, syllables not fit for ordinary men to bear. Chup went down the curving stair, and before him the increasing light carried a hint of the color of gold.

As he had been instructed, Chup counted the turnings of the stair, and stopped on what should be the last, before the source of light ahead could come into his view. There he drew in his breath, and said, clearly and loudly, pausing after each word, the three words of the incantation.

With the first word, there fell a silence in the air, where before he had only thought the air was silent; there had been a certain quiet murmuring that he was not aware of until it ceased.

With the second word, the light in the room below was dimmed, and the air became fresh and ordinary, where before he had only thought that it was so; and time began to make itself felt, so that Chup perceived the age in all the slimy stones that built the vault surrounding him.

The third word of the incantation seemed to hang forever on his tongue, but when he had said it, time flowed on once more as it should. The golden light before him grew as bright as ever; a certain rippling watery reflection in it had been stopped so it was steady, where before he had only thought that it was so.

With that Chup went on down, walking into Som's treasure room through its sole entrance. The vaulted chamber was round and high, perhaps twenty meters across. The golden light came from the center of it, seemingly from the treasure itself. It lay in careless-looking heaps, for the most part brilliant yellow metal, coins and jewelry, bars and foldings of gold leaf; here and there the piles were studded with the sharper glint of silver or the brighter flash of gems.

The treasure was still sealed from Chup by a last encircling fence, of what seemed fragile metal wands. He had no need to cross that barrier or worry about it. Instead he looked up at once to the upper vaulting of the high chamber. By the light of the ensorceled treasure, he saw that up there the seven guardian demons hung, where Hann's three words had sent them, like malformed bats in fine gray gossamer robes. They were head down, with arms or forelegs—it was hard to specify—that hung below their heads. Several of the dangling limbs hung nearly to the level of Chup's head, so elongated were the demons' shapes. One had a gray blur of a talon run like a fishhook through the hide of small furry beast, a living toy that struggled and squeaked incessantly to be free, and very slowly dripped red blood. As Chup watched the demons, they began to drone, like humans newly fallen asleep who start to snore.

With a shudder he pulled his gaze down and stepped forward. He stood staring for just a moment in awe at the accumulated wealth before him. He thought he had seen riches before, and owned some too. But he had known only handfuls compared to this.

The moment of distraction passed; what drove him had far more power over him than greed. Taking now from his pocket the golden circlet of Charmian's hair—infinitely brighter in his eyes than any hoard of metal—he held it up before him in both hands. He was reluctant ever to let it go. But after all it was the woman he wanted, not her token. It was for the sake of their future life together that he must give away the charm; for no other reason could he have parted with it now.

He tossed it from him, over the innocent-looking fence of fragile rods, toward the piled-up wealth. As it passed from his fingers it seemed to draw from him a greater spark than ever man might get by rubbing cloth and amber; and with this spark, invisible for all its power, Charmian's image in his mind was smashed and shattered as in a broken mirror.

Under the blow, Chup lurched forward two steps, hands outstretched and groping. Like one aroused from sleep-walking he blinked and cried out incoherently. His case was all the worse for his remembering all the nightmare that had brought him here; nightmare magic, that had made him trust his bride . . .

Tightly he squeezed shut his eyes, forgetting for the moment even the dreaming, droning, blinded demons over his head as he tried to call back Charmian's face. He visualized her now as beautiful as ever. But now, freed of the potent charm, he recognized her beauty as nothing but a mask worn by an enemy.

He stood gazing dazedly through the fragile-seeming fence of wands. The gold circlet had vanished, lost in the dazzle of the yellow metal stacked and strewn there . . . and now that he was freed of it, he did not want it back. Nor her. She would be with Tarlenot now, or Hann, or someone else. And Chup realized that he no longer minded that.

The thought broke in upon him that she must have known he would be freed by tossing away the charm. Or did she think he was still bound to her and blinded by the simple magic of her attraction, like the other men she used? No, he never had been enthralled by her before he picked up the charm. She must have known that he would, at this point, be set free.

To do what? Where did his best interests lie? Was he now committed irrevocably to helping her against Som?

Remembering now her face and voice over the last few days, he concluded that she still hated him for not being manageable without magic, especially for once slapping her to put an end to a mindless hysteria of noise. Was she done with using him now, and was her revenge already set?

At best his time of safety here was passing quickly. Cautiously he turned to leave the treasure chamber.

Above his head the little furry animal still writhed and squeaked, impaled upon the demon's dangling talon. Chup put up a hand in passing to rob the demon of its toy; he tossed the small beast ahead of him up the curving stair. There it might find a crevice in which to die in peace. The curses of three thousand wizards on all demons! He could not slay them, but he would take the chance to rob one of a toy. When he had climbed round the first turn of the ascending stair he paused, and uttered in reverse order Hann's three words. The light changed subtly, down below, and no longer was there perfect silence.

When he had climbed to the darkened level of the centipede, he was glad that he had wasted no more time below, for already the beast was stirring. It was not moving yet, but trying to rise, its feet a-scratching on the pavement in the darkness. He waited briefly, to give his eyes a better chance to see.

Now that he had thought a little, it seemed to him that he would have no more usefulness to Charmian. No longer bewitched, he could do nothing for her that someone more manageable—Tarlenot—could not do almost as well. She hated Chup, he felt quite sure of that, and she was not the girl to leave her hate unsatisfied.

He could see the dim shape of the centipede now, lying on its side, curling and uncurling like a slow snake swimming in the dark. Its feet scraped but were not yet ready to support it. Chup moved in the utmost silence, stepping toward the place where they must let down the ladder for him . . . here? Would this be where Charmian meant for him to die?

The more he thought, the likelier it appeared. This whole scheme could have been accomplished in a different way. Hann could have given the two deformed guards dried fruit, and magic words. They could have taken the circlet in and thrown it on the pile as easily as Chup. Except in that case Chup would have been left above ground, live and active, and with his own will back again.

Holding his breath, he listened for any sound above. They must be standing silent and listening too. Suppose he called up for the ladder and they lowered it. When he, unarmed, climbed to the top, the two Guardsmen would be there, one on each side, with weapons drawn . . . or suppose they did not lower the ladder, but laughed at him. They could have some means to grapple his body and hoist it up, after the centipede had struck him. Either way, once he was dead, put him down a crevice somewhere. He would vanish, or seem to be the victim of an accident or some chance quarrel or casual assassination—only there would be nothing to connect him with the treasure vault.

Behind Chup now, the sounds of the centipede grew louder. Looking back, it saw it was now managing to drag itself along the floor. It moved in his direction.

And close above him now he heard the faint sound of a sandal-scrape, and the intake of a nervous breath. "Where is he?" came a Guard's low whisper. "If the demons took him after all, they're certain to report him. Then we're through!"

Chup's eyes had now adapted well enough for him to see the beast in some detail. Thin as an arm its body was, though longer than a man, about as long as the many-weaponed tail that flicked and twitched behind it. A man with good arms might easily break the beast's thin neck, it seemed. Except that as soon as he tried to get a grip that tail would come snapping like a whip in the gloom, impossible to block or dodge . . . the clustered poison-spines grew longer than fingers on that tail. How could a man fight such a thing barehanded?

Why, thus, and so. And he would have a fighting chance, if it was dazed and slow. The cold calculation of tactics led Chup on into the outline of a larger plan. He trusted what his instinct told him, in a fight; the reasons came clear later, if he took the time to think them out.

The animal was trying now to stand, was on the verge of success. Chup drew a deep breath and moved into action. He scraped his sandals on the paving, making hurried footsteps, and in a low clear voice he called out: "Let down the ladder."

From up above, the laughter came.

The centipede was still sliding toward Chup, with a whispery scraping of its feet and body on the stones. Moving more quietly than the dazed beast, Chup circled to its rear and closed in. He grabbed in the near darkness with his unprotected hand for the tail, and caught it, just under the cluster of poison-spines at the tip. He set his foot against what might be called the creature's rump and shoved it down and pinned it when it would have tried to rise. Holding the tail straight was easy enough, but the multitude of slender legs had strength in numbers, resilient power surprising for their size. He was in for a struggle as soon as the drug had worn off completely, the more so as he must not kill this beast. The fighter's intuition on which he relied had grasped that point at once, though he had not thought it through with conscious logic: he must keep for himself the option of making Charmian's plan succeed or fail. To leave this animal dead would mean alerting Som and the plot's eventual discovery.

Up above, the Guardsmen's low voices were cheering on the beast.

"Put down the ladder, quick, by all the demons!" Chup cried out. Out of sight of those above, he was now sitting on the body of the beast to hold it down. His right hand was still vising the tail, his left hand feeling for the neck.

"Fight it out, oh great Lord Chup!" called down a voice. "What's wrong, did you forget your sword?"

He answered with a wordless cry of rage, as he shifted his grip upon the creature just slightly and stood up, lifting it across his shoulders. The weight was quite surprising for the size, it must be half as heavy as a man.

"That sounded like it did for him."

"It must have. Wait a moment, though."

The hundred legs remained in agitation, pounding softly, coldly, at Chup's head. He moved with his hideous burden, carefully keeping out of direct sight of the men above, stepping soundlessly.

One of the hidden voices said: "Toss down a bait. We've waited long enough. It got him, or he'd still be running."

Said the other, doubtfully: "He might have gone back down to the vault."

"Dimwit! The words won't work twice in one night, remember? Hann told us that. No man'll run to a wakeful demon, not even if a hundred-legger's chasing him. Throw a bait, we don't know when an inspector's going to come."

"All right, all right. Where's the beast? I'll toss one before his nose."

Chup twisted his burden off his shoulder and lowered it carefully in straining arms, just enough to let the little feet make scratching sounds upon the floor.

"There, there, hear it?" Chup heard the tiny spat of Hann's dried fruit, landing a meter or so before him. He waited, counting slowly to ten, his captive's body prisoned now under his left arm, its deadly tail still clamped safely by his tireless sword hand. Then he pressed the hundred legs down on the pavement once again, and this time let the writhing sides make contact too, to make the sounds of staggering and collapse.

"It took the bait. Go down."

"*You* go down, if you're in such a hurry. Wait till it falls, I say."

Chup lifted the animal again, and moved silently to a new position.

"It's quiet now. Go down and haul out the mighty

Lord Chup.''

''We had it settled, you were going down!''

''You're the stronger, as you always brag. So now be quick about it.''

A snarl of fear and anger.

''Quick! What if an inspector comes?''

It was the dwarf who eventually prevailed; the tall scarred man came down the ladder, slowly and hesitantly, frowning into the shadows where he thought Chup and the beast must both be lying. He had his sword drawn, and he spun round quickly when he heard Chup's soft step behind him. Then he screamed and jumped away and fell when he saw what weapon Chup was brandishing.

Without hesitation Chup turned and charged up the ladder, the writhing beast held above him and in front of him. He saw the dwarf's face, peering down incredulously, then tumbling backward out of sight in terror.

The dwarf was far too late in trying to draw his stubby sword. Chup by that time had reached the ladder's top, pitched the animal back down the hole, and was reaching for the little man. The dwarf's thick sword arm, caught, was twisted till the weapon clattered to the floor, then he himself was flung away across the room.

''Hold back!'' Chup barked out, with his back against the door. ''I mean no killing here, no valkyries buzzing down the tunnel to haul you out and bring investigators. Now hold back!''

The disarmed dwarf was sitting, scowling, where he had been tossed, and gave no impression of any eagerness to attack. Nor did the tall, scarred man, who, having beaten the maltreated centipede to the ladder on one lap or another of what must have been a lively race, now halted at the ladder's top. The tall one was armed, but so now was Chup, who had scooped up the dwarf's sword; and what Chup had just accomplished without a blade must have augmented his reputation considerably in the present company.

The men held back. Chup nodded, and reached behind him with one hand to slide back the massive bolts that sealed the door. "The scheme you were enlisted for goes forward, and if you play your parts I will see to it that you are rewarded." *As you deserve*, he thought. He went on speaking, with his field commander's voice: "The plan goes on, but now *I* am in charge, and not those who first bribed you and instructed you. Remember that. Raise that ladder."

The tall man hesitated briefly, then jumped to obey, sheathing first his sword. The dwarf was snuffling now like some schoolboy caught in an escapade.

Chup demanded: "What were you to do next? What signal were you to give her, that I am dead?"

The tall one said: "Your . . . your body, lord. To be left where it would be found; as if some feral centipede had . . . there are some in these caverns. To make your death look accidental."

"I see." Chup could now take time to think. "Maintain your guard here as if nothing had happened. If an inspector comes, say nothing. I left no traces down below. I will be back, or will send word, to tell you what to do." Now he could see the logic and the details of his plan, and he was grinning as he went out and shut the door.

VI

Be as I am

———◆—◆—◆———

The corpse's face had been shattered into unrecognizability, as if by a long fall onto rock, and the appearance of the rest of the body suggested that it had been nibbled by some kind of scavenger; reptiles, perhaps. The soldiers who had brought the body to Charmian—led by two officers who were not of her small group of plotters—stood by watching stolidly, as she attempted to make the requested identification.

She looked long at what had been the face, and at the heavy limbs that had once been powerful. They did not seem to have anything to do with Chup, but in their present state they might be his as well as not. Charmian was not squeamish about death—in others—and put out a hand and turned the ruined head. The build and hair color of the dead man were Chup's, and the tattered black uniform might be. She could see no marks of weapons on the body.

Half a day after Chup had set out upon his mission for her, she had sent word to Som's chamberlain inquiring whether her husband had been detained on any business. Word came back that nothing was known of his whereabouts. Half a day after that, the search was begun in earnest. Now another day later, this. Events were proceeding as she had planned.

"Where was this man found?" she asked.

"Wedged in a deep crevice, lady, in one of the deep caves. He might have fallen from a bridge." The officer's voice was neutral. "Can you make an identification?"

"Not with certainty." She lifted her eyes calmly; no one high in the councils of the East would be expected to show much grief for the loss of any other. "But yes, I think this is the body of my husband. Tell the Viceroy Som that I am grateful for his help in searching. And if it was no accident that killed the Lord Chup, then those who did it are as much Som's enemies as mine."

The officers bowed.

And half a day after they and their men had gone, wheeling their gruesome charge upon a cart, other messengers came from Som, more cheerfully garbed and with far merrier words to speak—it was a summons for her, to appear before the viceroy, but it came couched in the welcome form of gracious invitation.

Soon after those emissaries also had departed, leaving her time for preparation, the wizard Hann sat watching Charmian. They were in a central room of her elaborate suite. Hann sat a-straddle of a delicate chair turned back to front, his sharp chin resting broodingly upon his wiry, somehow unwizardly forearms, crossed upon the chair's high back.

The clothes that Charmian was to wear, close-fitting garments of raven black, hung thin and shimmering beside a screen. She herself, swathed in a white robe and soft towels and newly emerged from her bath, sat primping before an array of mirrors. She would make an imperious motion of her finger or her head, or merely with her eyes, and Karen or Kath would jump to adjust the angle of a mirror or lamp, or Lisa or Portia would fetch a different comb or brush, jar or phial, most of which their lady considered and rejected. Samantha was upon some errand for Charmian, and Lucia had earlier been judged guilty of some gross error and was not here; there was blood drying on the small silvery whip that lay at one end of the long dressing table. Charmian's face, utterly intent on appraising itself in all its multiple reflections, was for the time devoid of youth and softness, was ageless as ice and equally as hard.

Hann, observing her thus disarmed and charmless, was able to appraise her with something of the feeling he had when watching another magician pull off a perilous feat; professional respect.

He need never have worried about her nerves, he told himself. This girl-woman had matured considerably in the half year since she had come here as a frightened refugee. From the start she had been enormously ambitious; now she could be cold and capable, self-controlled. She probably could command an army, given a tactical adviser and mouthpiece to pass on orders—a man like Tarlenot. And she would have the nerve and ruthlessness to manage the other powers that were the viceroy's, even the power called Zapranoth—given the aid of a wizard of great skill, Hann.

The rulers of the Empire of the East would not care if Som were overthrown by one of his subordinates; that would mean only that a more capable servant had replaced a less. And now it did seem that Som's hand was faltering. (Only in the back of Hann's mind the question waited: why had the body been so mutilated, impossible to certainly identify? Well, why not? The Dwarf and Scarface swore that they had put the Lord Chup down a crevice as planned. And there were little scavenger beasts, that strayed out from the dungeons where they bred . . .)

Charmian was dismissing her attendants. As soon as the last of them had left the room she turned to Hann a questioning look. Hann, understanding, quickly made use of the best developed of his powers to quickly scan the suite and its environs. In this branch of magic he thought that he was unexcelled. The voices of invisible powers, inhuman and abject and faithful, muttered their reports to him, speaking close and softly so none but he could hear.

"Speak safely," he said to Charmian. "No one is listening but me."

Fingering a tiny perfume bottle, she asked: "How did our viceroy and master acquire his name?"

Hann was perplexed. "Som?"

"Who else, my learned fool? Why is he called 'The Dead'?"

He sprang up from his chair, aghast. "You don't know *that*?"

A light danced in Charmian's eyes. Looking at Hann in her mirrors, she was quite relaxed, save for her fingers on the little phial. "You know that I have met Som only twice, both times briefly. I realize of course that the purpose of his name must be to frighten those who hear it. But in what sense is it *true*?"

"In a very real sense!" Alarmed at her ignorance, Hann tilted his head from side to side in agitation.

"In a real sense, then. But tell mé more." Charmian's voice was soothing and deliberate, her eyes tranquil.

Hann absorbed some of her calm, turned his chair around, and sat down properly. "Well. Som does not age at all. He is immune alike to poison and disease, if what I hear is true." The wizard frowned. "He has reached some balance, struck some bargain with death. I admit I do not know how."

Charmian appeared to disbelieve. "You speak as if death were some man, or demon."

Hann, who had been to the center of the Empire of the East, said nothing for a moment. He had tied his fortune to this girl, and now her inexperience and rashness were beginning to frighten him. There was not time to teach her much. "I know what I know," he said at last.

She inquired, calmly enough: "And what else do you know of Som?"

"Well. I have never seen him enter battle. But it is said on good authority that any man who raises a weapon against Som finds himself smitten in that very moment with the same wound that he is trying to inflict."

On hearing this, Charmian's many mirror faces marred their foreheads with thoughtful frowns. "Then when I have put my ring of magic through Som's nose, and led him from his throne, how are we to do away with him? If no weapon can kill him . . ."

"There may be one."

"Ah."

"Though what the weapon is, I do not know. Nor does Som himself know, I believe." Through the powers that served him Hann had recently heard of recent threats to Som, by some mysterious power of the West, threats implying that the one effective weapon was known and would be used when the time came. "I do not know, but I could quickly learn, if I was given all the tools and wealth I needed for my work."

"When I am consort of a new viceroy, you shall have all you need and more. Now what else must I know of Som before I go to him?"

Hann went on worriedly:"There is sometimes the smell of death upon him; though when he is inclined to deal mildly with those around him, he covers up his stink with perfumes.

"And —I warn you. When you see him at close range and from the corner of your eye, you are liable to see not a man's face but a noseless skull. Can you smile and coo at that and not show your disgust?"

Once more she appeared to be concentrating completely on her reflection, adding a final something to her lips. "I? You do not know me, Hann."

"No! I admit that I do not." He jumped to his feet again and began to pace. "Oh, I know that you are able. But also that you are very young, and from the hinterlands. Inexperienced and untraveled in the world."

Her mirrors all laughed at him in light and easy confidence.

Annoyed, and worried all the more, he pressed on:"I know, back in your father's little satrapy, men were ruining themselves to win your favor. Some here, also . . . but remember that not everyone here will be so easily manipulated."

She gave no sign that she had heard.

He raised his voice. "Do you suppose you have enthralled and bedazzled *me*? I am your full partner in this enterprise, my lady. It is magic that is drawing Som to you; see that you do not forget it."

"You do not know me," Charmian repeated softly. And with that she pushed away her clutter of towels and jars and phials and turned to him from her mirrors. The room seemed brighter, suddenly. Even clothed as she was, in the loose concealing robe . . .

"Never have I seen . . ." said Hann, in a new, distracted voice; and after the four words fell silent, marveling.

She laughed, and stood up, with a single swaying of her hips.

Hann said in a blurred voice: "Wait, do not go just yet."

Her lips swelled in a pretended pout. "Ah, do not tempt me so, sly wizard. For you know how weak I am, how subject to your every trifling spell and whim. Only the knowledge that I must go, for the sake of your own welfare, enables me to tear myself away." And with that she laughed again, and vanished behind the screens where her attendants were, and Hann was left with no more than the memory of a vision.

By the time she had finished dressing and set out, the time of her appointment was near at hand, but she did not hurry; the audience chamber was not far off. On her walk deep into the citadel she was bowed on and escorted by a series of the viceroy's attendants, some of whom were human. Others were more beastlike or more magical than men, and had shapes not commonly encountered away from the Black Mountains. Charmian no longer marveled at them, like a backwoods girl; twice before she had walked this way.

At her first audience with Som, nearly half a year

ago, the viceroy had told her simply and briefly that it suited his purposes to grant her asylum. At her second audience she had stood silent and apparently unnoticed amid a number of other courtiers as Som announced to them the opening of a new campaign to recover the lost seaboard satrapies, and particularly to crush the arch-rebel Thomas of the Broken Lands; little or nothing had been heard of the campaign since then. On neither occasion had Som shown her any more interest than he might have bestowed upon an article of furniture. She had soon learned from the gossip of the other courtiers that he was dead indeed regarding the pleasures of the body.

Or so they all thought; what would they say today?

Looking into Som's great audience hall from just outside the door, she was vaguely disappointed to see that it was almost empty. Then as she was bidden enter by the chamberlain she saw that the viceroy had just finished talking with a pair of military men, who were now walking backward from his presence, bowing, noisily rolling up their scrolls of maps. Som was frowning after them. Charmian could not discern any change since her last audience in the man who sat upon the ebony throne. Som was a man to all appearances of middle size and middle age, rather plainly dressed except for a richly jeweled golden chain around his neck. He was rather sparely built, and his aspect at first glance was not unpleasant, save perhaps for his rather sunken eyes.

The soldiers backed past Charmian and she heard them stumbling and colliding with each other at the doorway as they left; but the viceroy's aspect softened as his eyes refocused on her.

The chamberlain effaced himself, and Charmian was alone with her High Lord in the great room where a thousand might have gathered—alone save for a few Guardsmen, heavily armed and standing motionless as statues, and for a pair of squat inhuman guardians—she could not tell at once if they were beasts or demons—that flanked his throne at a little distance on each side.

Som beckoned to her, with a gesture whose slightness she found enviable: that of one who knows he has complete attention. With humility in every move, her eyes downcast, steps quick but modest, she walked toward him. When still at a humble distance, she stopped, and made obeisance deeply, with all the grace at her command.

All was silent in the vast hall. When she thought it time to raise her eyes to the ebony throne, Som was gazing down at her, solemnly, with the stillness of a statue or a snake. Then like a snake he moved, with a sudden flowing gesture. In his dry, strong voice he said: "Charmian, my daughter—I have come to think of you as in some sense a relative of mine—you have lately begun to assume importance in my plans."

She dipped her eyes briefly and raised them again; so might a girl perform the gesture who had but lately begun to practice it before her mirror. A perfect imitation of innocence would never be convincing, here. "I hope these thoughts of me are in some measure pleasing to my High Lord Viceroy."

"Come closer. Yes, stand there." And when he had gazed upon her from closer range for a little while, Som asked: "Is it then your wish to please me as a woman? It is long since any have done that."

"I would please my High Lord Som in any way he might desire." There was perfume in the hall, of high quality certainly but stronger than the delicate scent she had put on herself.

"Come closer still."

She did so, and sank on one knee before him so close that he might have reached out a hand and touched her face. But he did not. For just a moment her nostrils caught a whiff of something else beneath the perfume; as if perhaps a small animal had crawled beneath the viceroy's throne and died.

"My daughter?"

"If you will have me so, my High Lord Som."

"Or should I say 'sister' to you, Charmian?"

"As you will have it, lord." Waiting for the next move of the game with her eyes cast down submissively, she saw (not looking directly at him) that Som had no nose, and that his sunken eyes were black and empty holes.

"My woman, then; we'll settle it at that. Give me your hand, golden one. In all my treasure hoard I have not such gold as you have in your hair. Do you know that?"

The statement gave her a bad moment of suspicion. But when she looked straight at her lord again, she saw an ordinary man's face, smiling thinly and nodding. However, she could not hear him breathe. And his hand, when she touched it, felt like meat that had been kept somewhat too long in the kitchen of a palace. Her hand did not for a moment tense, or her face change. She would take the fastest, surest way to power, though it meant embracing dead meat, and waking in the morning beside a noseless skull on a fine pillow.

In his dry voice, lowered now, he asked her: "What do you mark about me?"

Truthfully and without hesitation she replied: "That you do not wear the collar of the Guard, High Lord." It was a sign that Hann had mentioned, meaning that Som enjoyed some protection better than the valkyries.

The viceroy smiled. "And do you know why I wear it not?"

Impulsively she answered: "Because you are mightier than death."

He gave a silent, shaking grimace that was his laughter. He said: "You are thinking that it is because I am already dead. But yet I rule, and crush my enemies, and have my joys. Dead? *I have become death*, rather. No weapon, no disease, not even time, has terrors for me now."

She only vaguely understood him, and she could not think what to reply. Instead of speaking, she bowed her head and once more pressed to her lips the sticky tissue of his hand.

The viceroy said: "And all that is mine, my golden one, I have decided to share with you."

With unconcealed joy Charmian rose in response to the viceroy's tug on her hand. Som's dead hands pulled her to him, and she kissed him on the lips, or where lips should have been and seemed to be. "As your willing slave forever, gracious lord!"

Holding her at arms' length now, and smiling in great pleasure, he said: "Therefore you will become death too."

These last words of his seemed to stay circling like birds in Charmian's awareness, uncertain whether or not they meant to land. When at last they came fully home to her, her new triumph shattered like glass. Not yet did her distress show in her face or voice; her surface was her strength, where terror would reach only when it had already conquered all within.

She only asked, like a girl expressing sweet wonderment at a reward too great: "I shall become as you are, lord?"

"Even so," he assured her happily, patting her hand between his, with faint sticking sounds. "Ah, I could almost regret that such goldenness must perish at its peak, like the beauty of a blossom plucked; but so it must be, for the woman who shares my endless life and power."

With a shock of terror as sharp as the pain of blade or fire, she caught herself barely in time from trying to pull her hands away from his. In the back of her mind she was aware that other presences, human she thought, were coming into the audience chamber. But she could pay them no attention now.

She must express her joyful acceptance of Som's offer, without the least appearance of hesitation. But moment by moment her understanding of his meaning grew more certain and her fear grew more intense. Never for an instant had she expected this. She would rather die a thousand times, a million times, than become as he was. She could smile without a tremor at his dead face, she could embrace it warmly if she must. But to see the like of it in her mirror was unimaginable, was fear more pure than she had ever known.

No longer knowing whether she could conceal her horror, faint with the dizziness of it, she whispered: "When?"

"Why, now. Is anything the matter?"

"My High Lord—" Charmian could scarcely see. Would not some crevice open in the earth to swallow her? "It is only that I would preserve my beauty for you. That you may continue to enjoy it."

He made a gesture of impatience. "As I said, it is annoying that your appearance must be so much changed. But never mind. It is only mortal men who find those superficialities of great importance. What draws me to you is primarily your inner essence, so like my own—now, there is something wrong. What is it? Is the process causing you discomfort?"

"The process, my High . . .now? It happens to me now?" She was only half-aware of losing control, of pulling free from him and moving back a step.

He peered at her in evident astonishment. "Why, yes. I am impatient. Once having decided that you should rule beside me, I had the magicians begin the process of your transformation as soon as you entered the chamber. Already the change is far advanced—"

There was a rushing passage of the world, and screaming. Vaguely Charmian realized it was herself who screamed, and that the sound of pounding steps on wood and stone came from her own running feet. She had no longer any plan, no thought except to flee the death that moved and spoke and would engulf her with its own decay. A tall shape loomed before her, very near; she had run into it and rebounded before she saw it was a man, and knew his face.

The living face of Chup.

Still mad with panic, she tried to run around Chup, but he caught her by the arm. She had never seen his face so hard, not even on that day so long ago when he had slapped her. Now his voice came as if ground out between two stones: "Does it surprise you, Queen of Death, to see that I am still alive?"

Then Charmian understood what Chup's presence here must mean, that all her plotting had been discovered, her hopes destroyed. Her fear was so extreme she could not move or speak; she sank down in a faint before attendants came to carry her from the chamber.

Som, relaxed now upon his throne, spent a little time in the enjoyment of his almost silent, grimacing laughter. Chup waited, standing motionlessly at attention, until the viceroy had composed himself and beckoned him to come nearer.

"My good Chup, all your warnings to me have been borne out by investigation. The wizard Hann has been arrested. The circlet of the lady's hair has been found where you left it, in my treasure vault, with no trace visible of how you put it there. Needless to say, my security measures will be extensively revised. Fortunately, I am less susceptible to love-charms than these unhappy plotters thought; so it was shrewd of you to cast your lot with me."

Chup bowed slightly.

Som went on. "Unhappily, the man Tarlenot has departed on a courier's mission, on Empire business; it may be difficult to get him in our grasp again. But he left behind him his Guardsman' collar, which shall be yours, along with some substantial military rank."

For the first time since entering, Chup allowed himself to smile. "That's how I'd choose to serve, my High Lord Som. I am a fighter, with little taste for these intrigues."

"And you shall have your command." The viceroy paused. "Of course there is one matter first—your pledging to the East."

Ah, said Chup to himself, without surprise. I might have known.

Som continued: "When you were a satrap in our service, unlike others of your rank, you never came here to make a formal pledge. That has always seemed to us rather odd."

There was no satisfying the powers of the East. Always the certainty of great success was one more step away. Chup said, rather wearily: "I have been six months a crippled beggar."

"You were a satrap, free to come, for a much longer time than that." Som's voice was no longer so relaxed. "Before you lost your satrapy."

There was no good answer Chup could give. As a satrap, he had certainly been busy fighting, and he had told himself that he served his masters better in that way than by partaking in mysterious rituals. But they had never seen it exactly that way.

Now Som was looking at him from his sunken eyes, and Chup thought that he could smell the death. The viceroy said: "This pledging is more important than you seem to realize. There are many who ask to bind themselves completely to the East, to share in its inner powers, and are not allowed to do so."

As a soldier long accustomed to orders and the ways of giving them, Chup understood that there was now but one thing for him to say. "I ask to be allowed to make my pledge, High Lord. As soon as possible."

"Excellent!" Som took from around his own neck a richly jeweled chain, which he tossed carelessly to

Chup. "As a mark of my good favor, and the beginning of your fortune."

"Thanks, many thanks, High Lord."

"Your face says there is something else you
want."

"If I may retain for the time being the lodgings of
that treacherous woman. And her servants, those
who had no part in her plotting."

Som assented with a nod. The chamberlain was
evidently signalling him that other business
pressed, for he dismissed Chup with a few quick
words. After backing deferentially from the
chamber, Chup hung the chain of Som's favor
around his neck, and made his way to what had
been Charmian's apartment. With the chain around
his neck, he was now saluted by soldiers of the
common ranks. People of more standing, some of
whom had not deigned to notice him before, now
nodded or eyed him with respect and calculation.

When he reached the apartment he found it
swarming with men and women in black, each of
whom bore a skull insignia upon his sleeve. In the
past Chup had noticed only a few of these uniforms
and had not thought of their significance. They
were searching Charmian's rooms, thoroughly,
leaving casual wreckage in the process. Chup did
not attempt to interfere until he found their leader,
whose sleeve bore a much larger skull. This woman,
though she maintained an air of arrogance, was like
everyone else impressed with the chain that hung
about Chup's neck. In answer to Chup's question,
she led him to a service passage in the rear of the
apartment. There waited Karen, Lisa, Lucia, Portia,
Samantha, and Kath, chained together and huddled
against the wall.

Chup said: "You may release them, on my word. I
am to occupy these rooms, and I will require a good
staff, familiar with the place, to restore order from
this mess that you have made."

"They have not been questioned yet," the leader of the skulls said, finality in her voice.

"I am somewhat aware of how the plotting went, and who was involved, as our Lord Som can tell you. These were innocent. But they will be here when you want them for your questions."

It took a little more argument, but Chup did not lack stubbornness and pride, and there was Som's favor hanging down upon his chest. When the searchers in black at length departed, the six girls, unchained, were left behind. When they were alone with him the six of them came slowly to surround Chup. They said nothing, did nothing but gaze at him.

He bore this silent, disturbing scrutiny only briefly before issuing curt orders for them to get to work. The shortest, Lisa, turned away at once and started in; he had to bark commands, and kick a couple of the others, to get them moving properly. Then he walked out into the garden, turning ideas over in his mind.

On the next day Som's chamberlain came to Chup, and led him down into the mountain. Through devious and guarded tunnels they passed, until the tunnel they were in broke out into the side of a huge and roughly vertical shaft. This chimney had the look of a natural formation; it was about ten meters wide here, at a level well below the citadel. It seemed to widen gradually as it curved upward through the rock. Sunlight came reflecting down through it, from what must be an opening at the unseen top, beyond a curve. A precarious ledge winding round the inside of the shaft, made a narrow pathway going up and down. At the level where Chup and the chamberlain now stood, this ledge widened, and from it several cells had been dug back into the rock, and fitted with heavy doors.

Only one of these doors was not closed. Gesturing at it, the chamberlain, as if imparting necessary information, said: "In there lies she who was the Lady Charmian."

When Chup had nodded his understanding of this fact, if not of its importance, the chamberlain said quite solemnly: "Come." And started down the rough helix of a path that wound both up and down the chimney.

Chup followed. The two of them were quite alone on all the path, as far as Chup could see, peering down a long drop. From below, round a lower curve in the gradually narrowing chimney, in regions where the daylight scarcely reached, there came up a roseate glow. "Where are we going?" Chup asked the silent figure ahead of him.

The chamberlain glanced back, with evident surprise. "Below us dwells the High Lord Zapranoth, master of all demons in the domain of Som the Dead!"

Chup's feet, that had been slowing down, now stopped completely. "What business have we visiting the Demon-Lord?"

"Why, I thought you understood, good Chup. It is the business of pledging. Today I will explain how your initiation is to be accomplished. I must take you nearly to the bottom, to make sure you are familiar with the ground."

Chup drew a deep breath. He might have known they'd put demons into this, the one peril that could make him sweat from only thinking of it. "Tell me now, what is the test to be?"

He listened, frowning, while the chamberlain told him. On the surface of it, it sounded easier than Chup had expected. He'd have to face Zapranoth, but not for long and not in any kind of contest.

But there was something—wrong—about it.

Still scowling, Chup asked: "Is there not some mistake in this? I am to serve Som as a fighting man."

"I assure you there is no mistake. You will not suffer at the hands of the High Lord Zapranoth if you do properly what you are sent to do."

"I don't mean that."

The chamberlain looked at him blankly. "What, then?"

Chup struggled to find words. But he could not make it clear in his own mind what was bothering him. "The whole business is not to my liking. I think there must be some mistake."

"Indeed? Not to your liking?" The chamberlain's haughty glare could have withered many a man.

"No, it is not. Indeed. Something is wrong with this scheme. *Why* am I to do this?"

"Because it is required of you, if you wish to participate fully in the powers of the East."

"If you cannot give me any more definite reason, let us go back to Som, and I will question him."

It cost Chup some further argument, and the nearly incredulous displeasure of the chamberlain, but at last he was led upward again, and admitted to see Som once more.

This time he found the viceroy apparently quite alone, in a small chamber below the audience hall. In spite of half a dozen torches on the walls, the place seemed dim and cold. It was a clammy room, nearly empty of furniture except for the plain chair Som was sitting in, and the small plain table before him. On that table there stood upright mirrors, and at the focus of the mirrors a candle guttered, topped with a wavering tongue of darkness instead of flame, casting all around it an aura of night instead of luminance. Som's face turned toward the candle was all but invisible, and what little Chup could see of it looked less human than before.

In answer to the silent interrogation of that face turned toward him, Chup came to attention. In a clear voice he said: "High Lord Som, I have taken and given orders enough to understand that orders must be followed. But when I think an order is mistaken, then it is my duty to question it, if there is time. I question the usefulness of this initiation, in the form I am told it is to follow.''

Som the Dead was silent for a little time, as if such an objection were outside his experience, and he had no idea how to deal with it. But when he answered, his dry voice was hard to read. ''What is it you dislike about the pledging?''

''Excuse me, High Lord Som. That I dislike it is beside the point. I can carry out orders that I find unpleasant. But this . . . I see no benefit in this, for you, for me, for anyone.'' That sounded weak. ''Excuse me if I speak clumsily, I am no courtier . . . That's just it, High Lord. I am a fighter. What can a thing like this prove of my ability?''

Som's voice did not change; his face remained unreadable. ''Exactly what did my chamberlain tell you was required of you?''

''I am to take the woman Charmian from her cell. Tell her that I'm helping her escape. Then I am to lead her down into the pit, where dwells our High Lord Zapranoth. There I am to give her to the demon, to be devoured—possessed—whatever Zapranoth may do with human folk.''

The answer was quick and cold. ''The chamberlain spoke our will correctly, then. That is what we require of you, Lord Chup.''

A good soldier, if he had ever got himself in this deep, would know that this was the moment to salute, turn and leave. Chup knew it; yet he lingered. The hollows of darkness that were Som's eyes remained aimed at him steadily. Then Som said: ''The strong magic of a love-charm once bound you to that woman, but my magicians tell me you are free of that. What are your feelings for her now?''

In a flash of relief Chup understood, or thought he did. ''Demons! I'm sorry, lord. Do you mean, have I affection for her? Hah! That's what you're testing.'' He almost laughed. ''If you want me to feed her to the demons, well and good. I'll drag her to the pit and toss her in, and sing about my work!"

"In that case, what is your objection?" Som's voice was still cold and hard, but reasonable.

"I . . . High Lord, what good will it do to test my skill in lying and intrigue? To see if she believes me when I promise to help her? You'll have other men in your service far more cunning in such matters than I am. But you'll have few or none who'll fight like me."

"The test seems useless to you, then."

"Yes, sir."

"Does a good soldier argue all orders that seem to him useless? Or, as you said before, only those that seem mistaken?"

Silence stretched out following the question. Chup's stubborn dissatisfaction remained, but his will was wavering. The more he tried to pin down what was bothering him and put it into words, the more foolish his objections seemed. What harm could he suffer, in obediently carrying out this test, that could compare with all he stood to gain from it? Yet, encouraged by Som's seeming patience, he made an effort and tried once more to speak his inner feelings.

"This thing that you would have me do is small, and mean . . ." Then try as he might he could not form his shapeless revulsion any further. He made a weak and futile gesture and fell silent. Despite the clamminess of the chamber, sweat was trickling down his ribs. Now his coming here to argue seemed a hideous blunder. It wasn't that he cared what happened to her . . . the face of Som was growing hard to look at. And there were no perfumes here . . . but Chup was long used to the air of battlefields.

The viceroy shifted in his seat, and lo, was very manlike once again. The dark flame had burned down to only a spark of night. "My loyal Chup. As you say, your talents are not those of a courtier; but they are considerable. Therefore will I not punish you for this insolent questioning; therefore will I condescend this once to explanation.

"The test you do not like is given you *because* you do not like it, because you have shown reluctance to do things that you think of as 'small and mean'. To pledge yourself formally to the East is no meaningless ritual. In your case it will mean changing yourself, importantly, and I realize full well it can be very difficult. It is to do violence to your old self, in the name of that which you are going to become."

Time was stretching on in the odd little room. Like a man dreaming or entranced, Chup asked: "What am I going to become?"

"A great lord with the full powers of the East to call upon. The master of all that you have ever craved."

"But. How shall I change myself? To what?"

"To become as I am. No, no, not dead and leathery; I was playing with the woman when I told her she would be so. That is given only to me, here in the Black Mountains. I mean you shall become as I am in your mind and inward self. Now will you take the test?"

"My lord, I will."

"You are obedient." Som leaned closer, looking intently from his sunken eyes. "But in your case I wish for more than that. Loyal Chup, if you still had some affection for the woman, then merely to throw her to the demons might well suffice for your initiation. But as things are, it is not the woman, it is something else, within yourself, you must destroy ere you are ours completely."

Som rose from his chair. He was not tall, but he seemed to tower above Chup as he leaned yet closer, with his smell of old death. "You must be for once not brave, but cowardly. Small and mean, as you describe it. It will be difficult only once. You must learn to cause pain, for the sake of nothing but causing pain. Only thus will you be bound to us entirely.

Only thus will there be opened for you the inner secrets of power and the inner doors of wealth. And how can I give command of my Guard to one who is not bound to me and to the East?"

"The Guard . . ."

"Yes. The present Guard commander's aged and scarred well past his peak of usefulness. And you know Thomas of the Broken Lands, who is planning to assail us here, you know him and how he thinks and fights."

Not only an officer, but once again the commander of an army in the field . . . "My High Lord, I will do it! I hesitate no more!"

When Chup had gone, the viceroy returned to brooding on his other problems. What power was it, almost equal to his own, that dwelt in the circlet of gold hair and almost awoke in him the old desires of life?

His wizards would find out, in time.

In all their divinations lately, a threatening sign, the name of Ardneh, loomed up from the West. A name, with nothing real as yet attached to it. But it was in that sign, they said, that the Broken Lands and other satrapies along the seacoast had been lost . . .

VII

We Are Facing Zapranoth

———————◆◈◆———————

Thomas had been right about the reptiles, Rolf was thinking now, as he trudged up a small hillock to where his commander stood looking upward at the black, night-shrouded cliffs. Rolf's breath steamed in the air before his face. The onset of winter's chill, more noticeable at this altitude than it had been near the seashore, had kept the reptiles close to their roosts, had prevented their scouting out the army of the West during the days as it lay hiding in a hundred fragments. Night by night they had crept closer to Som's citadel.

Rolf reached the spot where Thomas stood, alone for once, his head tipped back. There seemed little to be seen, gazing upward, except the stars above the cliffs, whose tops seemed but little below the twinkling sparks.

"I think it's going to work," Rolf reported. He had recently been given his first command, a work party to set in order and inspect the balloon-craft that the djinn produced. All through this night the technology-djinn had labored at Gray's direction, making airships. Loford and the other wizards had concentrated on preventing the army's discovery by demon or diviner dwelling on the cliffs above.

Gray had now learned to manage the djinn successfully, Rolf reported. At the foot of the cliffs were twenty balloons tugging gently at their mooring ropes, each of the twenty capable of carrying five armed humans. The balloons were to ascend connected in pairs by stout lines, and longer cords would fasten each pair to the ones behind it and ahead, so the hundred riders would find themselves together at the top.

"Once we begin it, it had better work," said Thomas, nodding, when Rolf had finished detailing his report. Thomas himself was one of the hundred ascending by balloon to seize a foothold on the cliffs. Rolf was going up, to order the maneuvering and landing of balloons, and Gray, as wizard and technologist both. The other ninety-seven had been hand-picked from the fiercest warriors. At first Thomas had contemplated lifting his whole army in an aerial assault. But testing and maneuvering, by night and day, on various smaller cliffs between here and the Broken Lands, had dissuaded him. The number of things that could go wrong had proven almost limitless, and the time available for practicing was not. In maneuvers, the stunt had been worked successfully with as many as fifteen balloons. He had decided to risk twenty to seize the upper ending of the pass.

Thomas now had nothing more to say. Rolf, who had known him from his earliest days of leadership—not so long ago—wanted to offer more encouragement, but hesitated to interrupt what might be a necessary pause for thought. The pause was not long before Thomas turned suddenly and strode off down the hill. Rolf hurried after.

Most of Thomas's other officers were waiting for him, in a body, and he strode in among them briskly. "All here who are supposed to be? Once more: our flares will burn with a green fire, to signal you to start to climb the pass. We'll sound horns at the same time, as we've rehearsed. Once you get the word, by sound or light or both, that we've seized the top of the pass, come up as if a hundred demons were behind you."

"Instead of waiting for us at the top, aye!" There were sounds of nervous laughter.

Gray's tall figure loomed up. In one hand he

raised what appeared to be an ordinary satchel. "The demons at Som's command number far fewer than a hundred. And I have the lives of two of the strongest of them in here."

"Zapranoth? Zapranoth's life?" The murmured question came from several at once.

Gray, perhaps irritated, raised his voice slightly. "These are the lives of Yiggul, and of Kion. I have had them in my possession for some time, though for the sake of secrecy I have said nothing about them until now. And I have let them live, so I can destroy them when Som has called them up, thrown them into battle, and is depending on them. I am sure many of you know their names: they are both formidable powers."

There was silence.

Gray lowered his satchel. "You will see me blow them away like clouds of mist, before they have had time to do us the least harm."

"Not Zapranoth's life," one low-voiced listener said.

"No!" Gray snapped. "His life eludes us still. But these two are the strongest of the other demons. With these two gone, my brother and I can beat off the smaller fry like insects. We will not need the lesser demons' lives to drive them off."

There was no comment.

Gray went on, a little louder still: "Then, with all the others gone, we will be free to deal with him. Myself, Loford, the other stout wizards here. Zapranoth is mighty, well, so are we. We will hold off him or any other power, until your swords have won the day."

"And that we will do," Thomas put in with great firmness. "Any questions? Remember what you've been told about the valkyries. Let's move, the light is coming." He gripped hands all round with his officers, and led the way toward the moored balloons.

Rolf trotted to take his place in the basket of the leading balloon. He felt weak in the knees, as usual before a fight, but he knew that it would pass. It crossed his mind as he and Gray were boarding their separate balloons that he had never seen the wizard sleep. If Gray felt any fatigue from his night-long supervision of the djinn, he did not show it. Gray was compelling the djinn to accompany his balloon, and had even forced it somehow to dim the intensity of its fiery image; Rolf could see it like a floating patch of campfire embers in the shadow of the great hulking gasbag of Gray's balloon, some thirty meters distant. Tests had shown that the lifting gas provided by the djinn would not burn, but the problem of arrow-proofing the bags had not been entirely solved. They were protected to some extent by draped sheets of chain-mail whose rings were lighter than metal, made, as were the bags themselves, of something that the djinn called *plastic*.

Rolf had argued at some length for using to the full the tremendous powers of the djinn, delaying the campaign as long as necessary to exercise its abilities and try out the results; it seemed to him that in a few months enough Old World arms, armor, and techniques might be acquired and understood to give the army an overwhelming advantage against the East.

But Gray had vetoed such a plan. "For two reasons. First, not all Old World devices will work now as neatly and reliably as they did in the Old World. This is true in particular of certain advanced weapons. I do not fully understand why this should be; but I have my means of knowledge, and it is so."

"We could experiment—"

"With devices far more perilous than balloons? No, I do not think that we are ready. The second reason, and perhaps the stronger"—here Gray paused for a moment, looking round as if to make sure that he was not overheard—"is the chance that our djinn will perish in this battle. We are facing Zapranoth, and such a blow is far from impossible.

It would leave us without help in operating and maintaining our Old World weapons. No. Better that we fight with means we understand, depending on no one but ourselves."

Waiting now in the basket for the signal to ascend, Rolf grinned nervously at the impassive Mewick at his side. "Mewick, will you one day teach me to use weapons?" he asked in a low voice. It was something of an old joke between them, for Rolf at least. Mewick shook his head at Rolf in faint reproach and let his expression deepen into gloom.

The first balloons were loaded; the crews who were to do the launching were moving about briskly and capably in the gloom. Rolf did not see when Thomas gave the final signal for the attack, but those who were required to see did so. Two men standing by the mooring ropes each tugged and released a knot, and Rolf beheld the dim cliffside, ten meters from his face, begin abruptly to slide down in silence. Gray's balloon kept pace, its basket rocking gently, the dim fire of the image of the djinn suspended near it. The line connecting Rolf's balloon to Gray's drew gently taut, then slackened again. The longer lines, that the next craft were to follow up, were paid out from their reels outside the baskets.

The edge of sky that Rolf could see past the bottom of his balloon was now brightening with a hint of dawn. Higher the two baskets swung, moving in the perfect silence of a dream, emerging now from the deeper shadows at the base of the cliffs, so that the rocky walls before them rapidly grew more distinct. Turning for a moment to the west, Rolf could see the plains and desert, night-bound still, stretching far into vague, retreating darkness. His homeland, and the ocean, would be visible from here by day. But there was no time now to think of that.

Up and up . . .

Rolf's drawn sword snapped up in his hand to guard position, as the utter quiet was shattered by the strident cawing of a reptile. The creature had been dozing on the cliff face, a pebble's toss from the balloons, and it had wakened to see the strange shapes soaring past. Sluggish with chill, wings laboring, it came out in a dark, slow explosion from the rocks, and fled them upward strainingly. Mewick and others who had their arrows nocked were quick to draw and loose at it, and it was hit but not brought down. Clamoring all the louder, it flew on up above the great gasbags and out of sight.

From somewhere farther up there came a slow-voiced, cawing answer, and then another, higher yet. Then there was silence once more, until it almost seemed that the citadel might have returned to sleep.

Up and up. The men hanging in the baskets, straining to see and hear, had little to say to one another. Rolf found himself gripping the wicker rim, inside the quilted armor-padding, trying to lift the craft into a faster climb. He could see Gray murmuring to the djinn.

Rolf was expecting that at any moment they would top the cliff, but they had not done so before there came sure proof that the enemy had awakened. It was a small squadron of reptiles on reconnaissance. Their cawing and snarling was heard above, and then the soft thumps of their bodies striking atop the gasbags. The craft continued to rise steadily. The mail of plastic links had proven too tough for reptilian teeth and claws, and their bodies were not weighty enough to hold down the balloons.

When the reptiles flew down below the bags to find the baskets, arrows and slung stones bit at them accurately. They screamed and raged and fled; some fell, transfixed by shafts, turned into weights with fluttering fringes dropping through the brightening sky.

Now came the first sign that Som's fighting men were reacting to the attack. Rolf saw black-trimmed

uniforms running on ledges on the cliffs. A slung
stone thunked on the padding-armor right in front
of him, and he crouched lower. A fur-clad Northman
in Rolf's basket loosed an arrow in reply, and on the
cliff face a man dropped, toppled and slid on the
steep slope, trying to cling to it with the shaft in him,
plowing up a little avalanche.

Rolf knew they could not have much farther to
ascend, but still the top came as a surprise. The cliff
face fell back abruptly into a tableland, rough and
split by many crevices, but essentially flat. At the
rear of this horizontal reach, Som's low-walled
citadel sprawled, backed by the next leap upward of
the mountain. Across the little distance that separated his balloon from Gray's, Rolf heard the wizard
barking orders to the djinn. The two balloons, each
trailing a long spider-filament of line, slowed and
stopped their ascent just above the rim of the cliff.
Just here, almost beneath Rolf now, the narrow pass
delivered the road it had caught up on the plain
below.

Modest earthworks on one side of the debouching
road defended the pass against a climbing army,
and in fact formed the only real defense short of the
citadel's own walls. These works manned by half a
hundred men might easily hold the road, it seemed,
against Thomas's four thousand, so great was their
advantage of position. Ten or twelve men were in
the trenches now, pulling on black helmets and
gaping confusedly at the balloons. Their fortifica-
tion offered no protection against attackers dropping from the sky.

Gray was smoothly ordering the operations of the
djinn. Gas hissed from the bag above Rolf's head; the
basket he was riding skimmed rock, just in from the
cliff's edge. He pitched out a metal grapple on a line,
and leaped right after it. The balloon bobbed up
with the removal of his weight; for a moment he
stood there alone, the sole invader of Som's strong-
hold. But in the moment it took him to catch the

grapple and fix it in one of the many crevices in the
rock, Mewick was standing beside him, short sword
and battle-hatchet at the ready. Then with thudding
sandals others were landing, at their right and left.
Gray swung from his bobbing basket, agile as a
youth. Across ten meters of empty ground the ten
invaders faced the unfortified rear of the strong
point that looked so indomitably down the pass; ten
black-helmed Guardsmen, more or less, stared back
as if uncertain they were real.

Excepting Rolf and Gray, the aerial troops had
been hand-picked for guts and viciousness, and
those proved first in fighting skill had been selected
for the first balloons. The struggle for the earthwork
began without an order, in the space of one short
breath, and it was over in the time one might draw a
long breath and release a sigh; only one fighter of
the West had been cut down. Rolf sprang forward
with the rest, but all the enemy were slaughtered
before he had a chance to strike a blow. Still gripping his unmarred sword he turned to Gray; the
towering wizard with a motion of his arm was already sending out the signal of green fire, bright as a
small sun in the morning sky, leaping and shining in
the air above the pass.

Rolf turned and cried out: "Sound the horn!" A
Northman, blood from a scalp wound running in his
eyes, had the twisting beast-horn already at his lips;
he gave a nod, and winded it with all his might.

Sheathing his weapon, Rolf ran back to his balloons, made them secure with double grapples, and
deciding where the second pair should land. He was
none too soon, for they were close below and rising
rapidly. When they arrived, he helped to land them,
pulling on the thin ropes that the first balloons had
trailed, while their fierce passengers leaped out and
set themselves to hold the pass and landing place.
Rolf stayed at the landing place, seeing that the new
balloons were tied down, and looking for the next.
When he glanced toward the citadel, he heard

alarms and signals there, and saw folk running on
the walls, and reptiles in a sluggish swarm above
them. The main gates had been open, and still were;
at any moment a force must sally out to push the
Westerners from the cliff. Rolf looked the other way,
down the road that became a twisty ribbon marking
the bottom of the pass, but the army of the West was
still invisible. It would be hours before their legs
could bring them to this height.

In the earthworks, men had already methodically
separated the slaughtered Guardsmen's heads from
their bodies, gathered the freed collars and thrown
them down the cliff; the valkyries, coming down
from the high mountain, hovered and sniffed but
could find no one to save. Rolf and the others,
taught by Gray to expect the flying things, still
stared at them, Rolf with particular fascination.

"Demons!" someone called out. It was not an ex-
pletive, but a warning.

Faces turned to Gray. He had already seen the
disturbances in the air a little way from the citadel,
hanging low, more like the roiling of heat above fires
than like rainclouds. Opening his satchel, he pulled
out of it a flowery little vine, wrapped as if for suste-
nance around a piece of damp and maggoty wood.
In Gray's other hand was a silvery-gleaming knife.

As the two presences drifted nearer in the lower
air, sweeping reptiles in a timid swarm before them.
Gray brought the blade near the tender, innocent
green tendrils of the vine. He muttered a few words
in a low voice—and cut.

Silver flashed in the sky above the citadel, like a
reflection or mirage of an enormous axe. The blow
that struck one of the demons came in utter silence,
but was irresistible nonetheless; its image in the air
split in two spinning halves. Gray scarcely looked
up; his hands, those of a gardener, kept at their
work, severing and plucking leaf from stem, slicing,
splitting, and demolishing the vine. Gray breathed
upon the rotten wood, and green flame sprouted

from it. In unburned hands he held it up, watching the clean flame devour the clinging fragments of the petals, leaves and stems. "Yiggul," he said with feeling, "trouble our fair world no more." And he chanted verses in a language Rolf did not know.

Fire burned now in the sky as well consuming the scattered pieces of the demon. Its companion paused in his advance, but then came drifting on again.

"Now, Kion, let us say farewell to you." Gray reached into his satchel once more.

The roiling disturbance in the air, the size of a small house, shook for a moment as if with fear or rage, then came toward Gray like a hurled missile. Some of the men around the wizard threw up their arms or ducked their heads; others, just as uselessly, raised shield and blade. Gray shot forth his arm, and the object he had pulled from his satchel—it looked like some trinket of cheap metal—was held above the chunk of burning wood. The hurtling demon was transformed into a ball of glowing heat. Rolf heard, more in his mind than in his ears, a scream of pain beyond anything he had yet heard upon a field of war. Kion's course was bent from what he had intended. He struck the earth far from the Western men, spattering flames and rock about his point of impact, where he left a molten scar; he bounded up again, twisting and spinning like an unguided firework, and all the while the scream went on unbreathingly, and Gray's unburning hand continued to hold the bauble in the fire. The metal of it, tin or lead mayhap, melted in beautiful silvery drops that fell into the flame and there unnaturally disappeared. And as the bauble melted, so diminished the fireball that had been the mighty demon Kion, flashing madly from one part of the sky to another until it vanished in a final streak of brilliancy.

Gray pressed his hand down on the fiercely burning wood, and it went out like a candle. "What are these others here?" Gray asked in a low voice. "Do they propose to try our strength, after what we have just done?" Rolf saw that there were indeed a scattering of other disturbances in the air, man-sized waverings visible to him only now when the larger two were gone. He heard, or felt, the thrummings of their power. Alone, he might have fallen down or fled before the least of them. Standing here with Gray and Loford, now, he found he minded these minor demons no more than so many sweat-bees or mosquitoes. And now as if they had heard Gray's challenge, and chose not to accept it, the swarm of them began to disappear. Rolf could not have said just how; one moment the air above the citadel was thick with them, then they were fewer, and soon they were no more.

"So, then, masters of the Black Mountains," mused Gray, still in the same low tone of conversation, that you would not think was audible ten meters off. He stood straight, dusting his hands absently against one another. "So. Do you mean then to let our differences be settled by the sword? In the name of my bold companions here I challenge you: march out and try with blades to pry us from this rock!"

Rolf heard no answer from the citadel, only a shouting from behind him, where more balloons were ready to discharge their fighting men. He ran back to take charge of the docking. Thomas, in a gleaming barbut-helm, was arriving in the ninth pair of airships, a position he had hoped would allow him to oversee both ends of the operation.

When Rolf turned back toward the citadel he could see through the open gates that men were marshalling inside as if to sally out in strength. Confusion had been replaced by the appearance of purpose.

"Som is on the battlement," said someone. "See,

there. I think he wears a crown of gold."

Rolf shivered. The day was chill. Winter was near at hand, and this place was high.

"If he takes the field," warned Loford, "do not strike at him, but only ward his blows. The wound you would inflict on Som the Dead is likely to become your own to bear."

Gray, too was shivering, calling for a cloak.

Why should the sun seem dimmer, when there were no clouds? And Rolf had a feeling in his guts like that of being lost, alone, at night amid a host of enemies . . . and now, why should he think there mighy be something wrong with the mountain, that it might crumble and collapse beneath his feet? Loford, Thomas, all of them, were beginning to look at one another with dread.

Gray said softly: "Zapranoth is coming."

VIII

Chup's Pledging

———◆◈◆———

Chup nodded once to the expectant-looking jailor—who stood near the door of Charmian's cell. The man responded with a facial contortion that might represent a smile, and took two steps backward to a spot well shaded from the feeble glimmerings of dawn now probing down the demons' chimney. There he let himself down carefully and lay still. Only his feet remained clearly visible, like those of a man laid low by stealthy violence.

At the cell door, Chup paused a moment to try to seating of his new sword in its sheath, and give a loosening shake to the nerve-tight muscles of his shoulders. He thought in wonder that if he were plotting a real escape for Charmian, instead of this safe pledging trickery, he would not be quite as tense as this.

The heavy bar grated as he raised it from the cell door, and he reminded himself to strive more realistically for silence. Cautiously he turned in the lock the key he had been given. The massive door swung outward at his pull. Chup's shadow fell before him into the uncleanness of the cell. There Charmian huddled on the floor, wearing the same black clothing of her audience with Som, shimmering garments, slit revealingly, foolish now as rags would have been at the Emperor's court.

When she recognized Chup, the sharp terror in Charmian's face turned dull; she had evidently expected visitors even more menacing than he.

He stepped back from the doorway and said in a

low voice: "Come out, and quickly." When she did not move at once he added: "I'm going to try to free you."

The words sounded so utterly false in his own ears that it seemed impossible that clever Charmian could believe them for a moment. But she stood up and came toward him, though hesitantly at first. Her blond hair hung disheveled, half-concealing her face. Without a word she came out of the cell, and stood against the wall, her face averted, while Chup played the game of dragging the shamming guard into the cell and barring up the door again. Then at a motion of Chup's head she followed close behind him as he set foot upon the downward path.

They had gone down perhaps two hundred paces, when Charmian in a small voice broke the silence: "Where are we going?"

He answered, without turning. "We must go down, in order to get out."

Her footsteps behind him stopped. "But down there is where the demons nest. There is no way out, down there."

Startled, he too stopped, and turned. "How do you know? Have you come this way before?"

She seemed surprised by the question. "No. No, how could I have?" Still she was not looking directly at him.

"Then follow me," he growled, and started down again. After a moment her soft footfalls followed. She must believe his masquerade, or she would be screaming at him or pleading. But the evidence of success brought him no satisfaction.

Pretending to be cautious and alert, looking this way and that, pausing now and then as if to listen, he led her down toward the pit. He felt weary and awkward as if he had been fighting to the point of physical exhaustion. It will mean changing yourself, Som had said, you must do violence to your old self. Yet what Chup was supposed to do was basically quite simple, and on the surface there was nothing in it difficult for a bold man. He was to bring her down (by fair words and promises, not by force—that had been emphasized) to the Demon-Lord's chamber at the bottom of this hole. There where she expected a door to freedom he was to give her to the demon. And then he was to run away. If he did not run away, and briskly, the chamberlain had warned him, Zapranoth in his demonic humor might nip him too.

His pledging was a task for one who giggled and ran away, and Chup now liked it less than ever. He did not see how he could succeed, how Charmian could fail from one moment to the next to guess the truth. Well, let her. But no, she still followed him obediently. He realized suddenly how desperate she must have been, how ready to grasp at any hope.

His pretended alertness suddenly became real. From below, where all had been ominous silence, there arose now a murmuring strange sound which he did not at once identify but which he did not like.

The first whisper of it froze Charmian in her tracks behind him. "Demons!" she whimpered, in a voice of certainty and resignation.

Chup had been assured there would be no interference, no distractions, while they were going down. He took a step back, fighting his own fear of demons, trying to think. Thinking was not easy; the sound grew rapidly louder, and at the same time more plainly wrong. It put Chup in mind of the gasping of some unimaginable animal; it made him think of a terrible wind sent blowing through the solid earth.

Now there was light below, a pinkish glow, as well as sound. Chup could make no plan. As if seeking each other's humanity, by instinct he and Charmian put their arms around each other and crouched down on the narrow path. The sound was almost deafening now, a climbing clamor flying upward from the pit. With it came the aura of sickness that accompanied demonic power, an aura stronger

than Chup had ever felt before. The brightening
roseate light seemed to drive back the feebly growing glimmerings of the sun. He clenched his eyes
shut, held his breath—and the rush, as of a multitude of beings, passed by them and was gone.

"Demons," Charmian whimpered once more.
"Yes . . . oh, it seems that I remember them, rushing
by me in this place. But how?"

"What do you remember? Have you been down
this pit?" he rasped at her. He wondered if she was
planning some deception. But she only shook her
head, and continued to avert her face.

He pulled her to her feet and led her down the
curving path once more. What else could he do?
Daylight enough came trickling from above to show
the way. They came to a doorway, but when Chup
peered in there was nothing but an alcove, no way
out. No way out . . . but he must go on to pass his
pledging, to reach the power of the inner circles of
the East.

What else could he do? Down and down they
went, though very slowly now.

Soon it began again, the noise far down below
them, climbing fast.

"It is Zapranoth," said Charmian.

This time a bass quaver, that told of madness
rampant in the foundation of the world; this time
the whole world shuddered and sickened with the
coming up, and the light it cast before was blue and
horrible.

Charmian began to scream: "Lord Z—"

Chup grabbed her, stifling her mouth beneath his
palm, and cast himself and her once more down
upon the narrow curving ledge, this time at full
length, with both their faces turned toward the wall
of rock. With a twisting and a stretching of the uni-
verse, with impacts of great footfalls smiting air and
rock, the blaring, glaring Lord of Demons trampled
past them. If they were seen, they were ignored, as
two ants might have been.

Chup did not see the demon. His eyes had shut themselves, and at the moment of the demon's closest presence all his bones seemed turned to jelly. This must be Zapranoth. Against this, no use to think of showing bravery; compared to this, the demons rising earlier had been small. And the demon who, days ago, had entered his beggar's hovel to heal and threaten him—that one had been a nasty child making faces, nothing more.

When the world was still and sane and tolerable once more, he raised his head, gripped Charmian by the hair, and turned her face toward him. "How did you know that it was him? From far away, when first he started up?"

She looked convincingly bewildered. "I don't know . . . my Lord Chup, I do not know. By his sound? But how could I ever have heard him, met him, and forgotten it? You are right, I knew at once that it was he. But I don't know how I knew."

Chup got slowly to his feet. There was one small comfort: the game he was to play could not proceed until the Demon-Lord came back from whatever unforseen errand had called him out. Chup would have to find some means of stalling until then. But at the moment he could think of no plausible excuse for staying where they were. Slowly he led Charmian downward once again.

They had gone but two more turns around the gradually narrowing chimney when there came a different and more human sound, from far above. It was faint, but to Chup's ears unmistakable—the cry and clash of men at war. Chup listened, knowing now what had called the demons forth. No one in the citadel had thought it possible for Thomas to make a direct assault; well, it was not the first time he had been underestimated.

So the wait for Zapranoth might take some time, though it seemed likely that he ultimately would return triumphant. It was hard to imagine that Thomas could raise a power equal to the Demon-

Lord, even if he could get his army up the pass. Chup grinned the way he did when he felt pain. He led Charmian on down until they came to another doorway opening into another blind alcove. There he took her by the arm and pulled her in.

"What is it?" she whispered, terrified anew.

"Nothing. Just that we must wait a bit."

He expected her to ask him why, and wondered how he could answer. But she only stood there with her eyes downcast, face half-hidden by her hair. Surely this behavior was a pose, part of some plan she was evolving. He had seen her terrified before, but never meek and silent.

Considering what to do next, he sat down with his back against the wall, watching the entrance to their alcove. Almost timidly, she slid down beside him. In her new, small voice she said: "Lord Chup, when I was in the cell, I hoped it would be you who came for me."

He grunted. "Why?"

"Oh, not that you would come to help me, I didn't dare hope that. Even now . . . but I knew that if you came to take revenge, you would be quick and clean about it. Not like Som, not like any of the others."

He grunted again. Suddenly anxious to know what it would feel like now, freed of all enchantments, he pulled her near, so that their mouths and bodies were crushed together. She gasped and tensed, as if surprised—and then responded, with all her skill and much more willingness than ever before.

And he discovered that to him, the touch of her meant nothing. It was no more than hugging some huge breathing doll. He let her go.

To his surprise, she clung to him, weeping. He had never seen this act before; puzzled, he waited to learn its point.

Between her sobs she choked out: "You—you find me then—not too much changed?"

"Changed?" Then he remembered certain things,

that made her puzzling behavior understandable. "No. No, you are not changed at all. Our mighty viceroy was lying about the destruction of your beauty. You look as good as ever, except for a little dirt." For the first time in days Chup could hear his own voice as an easy, natural thing.

Charmian stared at him for a moment and dared to believe him. Her sobs changed abruptly into cries of joy and relief. "Oh, Chup, you are my lord—high and only Lord." She choked on fragments of strange laughter.

Feelings Chup had not known were his came fastening on him now like mad familiars. He could not sort them out or put them down. He groaned aloud, jumped up, and pulled Charmian to her feet. He seized her shoulders, gripping them until it seemed that bones might crunch, while she gasped uncomprehendingly. Then, still holding her with his left hand, he drew back his right and swung it, openpalmed but with all his rage. "That, for betraying me, for using me, for trying to have me killed!"

The blow stretched her out flat, and silenced all her cries. A little time passed before she stirred and groaned and sat up, for once ungracefully. Her hair no longer hid her face. Blood dripped from her mouth and there was a lump already swelling on her cheek. She finally could ask him, in the most dazed and tiniest of voices: "Why now? Why hit me now?"

"Why, better later than never. I take my revenge my own way, as you said. Not like Som, nor any of the others here." Gripping his sword hilt, he looked out of the alcove, up and down the spiral path. Let them come against him now, he was Chup, his own man, and so he meant to die.

When he saw no understanding in her dazed face, he went on: "Shake your head and get it clear. I was not to lead you out of this foul place. I was to play the court jester for Som and Zapranoth; thus should I prove my fitness to join the elite of the East. They will not have a free man's service. They must have pledgings, and grovelings, and for all I know, kissings of their hinder parts as well. *Then* will they open to their tested slave the secrets of power and the doors of wealth. So they say. Liars. Gigglers at cripples, and pullers of wings from flies. I know not if Som stinks of death—or only loadbeast-droppings!"

He felt better for that lengthy speech, and better still for the action that had just preceded it. Now there ensued a silence, while his breathing slowed and Charmian's grew steadier, and she ceased to moan.

And now once more he heard, from far above, the clash and cry of many men at arms.

Charmian, her voice now nearly normal, asked: "Is that Thomas's assault we hear? The one our generals thought could not be made?"

Chup grunted.

"They of the West bear me great hatred," Charmian said. "But if I've any choice I'll go to them instead of Som."

"You'd be wise, if you could do so. They in the West are living men, and many would fall down swooning at a flutter of your eyelids. What is it now?"

Some thought or memory had brought a look of new surprise into her face. "Chup. I have never been down into this cave before—and yet I think I have. Things as they happen seem familiar. The winding path, these alcoves. The sounds the demons make in passing, and the feelings that they bring—the wretched feelings most of all." She shivered. "But how can I have known them, and not remember plainly?"

His thought was practical. "If you have been in this cavern, or seen it in some vision, then remember a way out of it, that we can use."

She gave him a long, probing look, with something in it of her old haughtiness. Her bruised face did somewhat spoil the effect. "Have you finished now with taking your revenge on me?"

"I have more important things to think of. Getting out of here, now that I've spoiled my pledging. Yes, I'll help you out if you'll help me. But turn treacherous again, and I'll kick you down the pit at once."

She nodded soberly. "Then I'll help you all I can, for I know what to expect from Som. What must we do?"

"You ask me? I thought you might recall an exit from this hole. And quickly. While the battle's fierce, we're probably forgotten."

Doubtfully and anxiously she stared at him. "I think—whether it is memory or a vision that I have—I think that there is no way out for us below." Her voice grew dreamy. "At the bottom of this chimney there are only huge blind chambers in the blackened rock. And strange lights, and the demons roaring past. I would have run back, screaming, but my father gripped my—" She broke off with a little cry, her blue eyes widening.

"Your father led you down here? Ekuman?" Chup did not bother trying to understand that; if it was part of some new and elaborate deception, he could not see its point. He prompted: "How did you get out? If there's no way below, we must go up again. Where does the top of this shaft break out of the mountain?"

She had to make an effort to recall herself, to answer him. "I don't know. I don't think that I was ever at the top of this chimney. It seems to me we entered and left it at the level of the cells . . . Chup, why would my father bring me here?"

Not answering, Chup led her out of the alcove, and started on the long ascent, at a good pace. Little was said between them until they drew near the level of the cells again. Here Chup proceeded cautiously, but there was still no one else in sight. The

cell that had been Charmian's was once more unbarred and open. Every available man must have
been mobilized to fight; but how long that situation
might last was impossible to guess.

He gripped Charmian's arm. "You say you entered
and left the shaft here. Remember a way out of the
citidel that we can use."

"I . . . " She rubbed her head wearily. "I can remember no such way. We should go on to the top.
There must be some exit there, to sunlight if not
freedom."

Chup went up quickly. The sounds of combat
were noticeably louder here.

Still they met no one. The chimney straightened
to show them the gray-blue sky, over a mouth ringed
by ragged outcroppings of rock. The path seemed to
go right up to the mouth and out to unbarred freedom.

Chup and Charmian had only one more circuit of
the chimney to climb, to its outlet barely ten meters
above them, when there appeared there against the
sky the head of a man in Guardsman's helm and
collar, looking down. Before Chup could react, the
man had seen them. He called out something, as if to
others behind him, and withdrew from sight.

"Perhaps I should go first," suggested Charmian,
in a whisper.

"I think so." He would rather not try to fight his
way up this narrow path, against unknown odds.
"I'll walk a step behind you, as your aide." The men
above could not be certain of Chup's and Charmian's current power and status, not even if they
knew she was a prisoner last night. So things went in
the intrigue-ridden courts of the East.

Charmian ran combing fingers through her hair,
put on a smile, and took the lead. With Chup following impassively they marched another half-turn up
the chimney, which brought them into plain view of
the pathway's narrow exit at the top, and of the men
who guarded it. These were looking down with, to
say the least, considerable suspicion. There were

eight or ten of the Guard in view, and Chup noted with inward discouragement that they included pikemen and archers.

Anger in her voice, Charmian called up: "You there, officer! Why do you stare in insolence? Bring cool water to me! We have slipped and fallen and nearly killed ourselves upon your miserable path!" There must be an explanation of her soiled garments, and of Chup's anger marked upon her cheek and lip.

The faces of the soldiers turned from hard suspicion to noncommittal blankness. On Chup's breast the chain that Som had given him still swung, massive and golden, and he made sure it could be seen, at the same time he favored the officer with his best haughty and impatient stare.

The Guards officer—a lieutenant—softened considerably from his first hard pose. He could not keep his new perplexity from showing. "My lady Charmian. I had heard that you—" He shifted his stance. "That is, you or no one else is to be allowed to pass this way, according to the orders I have been given."

"The lady wanted a good look at the fighting," Chup said, guiding her forward with a touch. From the way some of the soldiers kept glancing over their shoulders he guessed that the action was in plain sight from where they stood.

The lieutenant protested. "Lord, why did you not watch from the battlement instead?" But he made no attempt to block their way. Instead he turned to one of his men, ordering: "Here, find some water for the lady."

Charmian and Chup had now come right up to the top of the path, and stood among the soldiers. They had emerged in the midst of the broken plain, roughly halfway between the citadel and the sudden drop-off of the cliffs. Looking out over a breastwork of piled rocks, they had a good view of the fighting, perhaps three hundred meters distant. The fight was not at the moment being carried on with blades, but it was none the less a deadly struggle. Holding the roadhead at the pass were some fourscore men of the West, Chup saw, along with the balloons that must have surprised the defenders. The Guard, or most of it, was drawn up on the plain in battle ranks, but only waiting now.

Above the ground between the battle lines, drifting, like some foul cloud of smoke, was Zapranoth. The power of the Demon-Lord was being turned away from Chup, but still he thought he felt its backlash here, and looked away toward the citadel. Small figures were on the parapet; he thought he could see Som. Above the fort, a single valkgrie droned toward its lofty home.

Charmian finished her thirsty drinking from a canteen handed to her by an awkward soldier. "Oh, captain," she now smiled, dabbing prettily at her sore lips, "I had heard you were a man of gallantry, and I believed it true, and I have climbed that horrible path to reach you. I wish to see the ending of the battle close at hand, not stand with all the timid females behind a wall. Surely if I go out a little way, a little closer, I will still be safe, with you and all these stalwart men of yours at hand?"

"I . . ." The lieutenant floundered, trying to be firm. It was so easy for her. Chup marveled in silence, shaking his head slightly while he took his turn at the canteen. Distant Guardsmen chanted a war cry, and somewhere a reptile cawed.

Charmian was going on. "We do not mean that you should leave your post. The Lord Chup will go with me, but a little way out upon the plain here . . . I will tell you the truth, there is a wager involved, and I feel I must reward you if you can help me win it."

The lieutenant had no more chance than if Chup had come upon him here unarmed and alone. In the space of half a dozen more breaths Charmian was being helped over the barricade of stones, her escorting lord beside her. As they walked out upon the empty, crevice-riven field that stretched away toward the fighting, he heard the reptile again, cawing somewhere behind them; and this time he thought he could make out a word or two within its noise. Chup took his bride by the arm, as if to steady her on the hazardous ground, and she heeded the silent increase of his fingers' pressure. They walked faster. With a stride and a stride and another stride, the barricade, the soldiers, and the power of the East fell meter by meter behind them. Not that the way in front was clear.

" . . . escaaaaped!" came the raw reptile cry, much louder now. "Rewaaards for their bodies, double reward for them alive! Trraaitor, Chup of the Northern Provinces! Prisoner escaped, Charrrmian of the Broken Lands!"

Chup ran, dodging with every second or third stride to spoil the archers' aim. Charmian, close behind him, screamed as if they had caught her already. Now ahead of him there loomed across his way a chasm, one of the splits that ran in deeply from the mountain's edge. It was too wide at this point for even a desperate man to try a jump. The farther Chup ran the more treacherously uneven grew the footing, and he dropped to all fours to scramble over it, even as an arrow sang past his ear. From the officer's bawled orders not far behind, he knew that close pursuit was right at hand. The reptile now shrieked in triumph right above him. Charmian cried out her panic with each breath, but her cries stayed right at Chup's heels.

He reached the edge of the deep crevice. To follow along it on this footing of broken, tilting rocks would be a slow and tortuous process, and the pursuit could not fail to catch up to easy arrow range at once. To jump across the chasm was impossible. To attempt to scramble down its nearly vertical side would have seemed at any other time like madness, but now Chup unhesitatingly began to slide and grab. Better a quick fall than the demon-pits below

the citadel. But all was not lost yet: on a slope this
steep there must be overhangs, to offer some protection against missiles from above; and Chup
could see now that at a distant bottom the crevice
ran out in a dry watercourse and got away from Som.

Chup swung from handholds, danced and
bounded, leaping down the slope. Another arrow
twirred past him, going almost straight down, and
after it the hurtling blur of a slung rock. He started
falling, slid and grabbed in desperation, and got his
feet upon a ledge that was not much wider than his
soles. A moment later he was clutched by Charmian
sliding down beside him and almost pulled into the
abyss. To his left the ledge all but vanished, then
widened into what looked like opportunity, a siza-
ble flat spot under a large overhang. With Charmian
still clutching at his garments, he lunged that way.
Somehow the two of them scrambled to that spot of
comparative safety, on footholds that would have
been suicidal if attempted with cold calculation.

They were sheltered from missiles on a flat space
big enough to sprawl on carelessly, while they
gasped for breath. Somewhere, ten or twenty meters
above them but out of sight, the lieutenant was
bawling out a confusion of new orders.

The reptile found them almost instantly. It hovered over the chasm on deft and leathery wings,
screaming its loathing and alarm, carefully staying
out farther than a sword might sweep. Charmian
with a wide swing of her arm threw out a fist-sized
rock; through luck or skill it caught a wing. The
beast screamed and fell away, struggling in pain to
stay in the air.

But it had already screamed out their location to
the men above.

Chup stood up and drew his sword and waited for
the men to come. From the renewed sounds of battle farther off, he soon picked out a closer sound, the
scraping and sliding of sandalled feet on rock, too
desperately concerned with footholds to be furtive.

"Both sides!" Charmian cried out. A man was sliding down toward them on each side of their almost cavelike shelter. But each attacker had to think first of his own footing. Chup put the first one over easily before the man could do more than wave his arms for balance, then turned quickly enough to catch the other still at a disadvantage. This one, going over, dropped his sword and managed to catch himself by his hands. Only his fingers showed, clinging stubbornly to the ledge, until Charmian, screaming, pounded and shattered them with a rock.

Chup sat down once more resting while he could. As Charmian knelt beside him, he said: "They'll have a hard time getting at us here. So they may just wait us out." He leaned out for a quick glance at the slope below them, it was worse than that above. "I don't suppose you got out by this route the last time you were here."

"I—don't know." Somewhat to Chup's surprise, she lost herself again for a time in silent thought. "I was only a child then. Twelve years old, perhaps. My father led us —" Her face turned up, wide-eyed with another shock of memory. "My sister and I. My sister. Carlotta. I have not thought of her from that day till this. Carlotta. I had forgotten that she ever lived!"

"So. But how did you get out? Not down this cliff somehow?"

"Wait. Let me think. How very strange, so many memories wiped out . . . she was six years younger than I. Now it comes back. My father took us both down the long spiral path. Into the demon chambers at the bottom. There . . . he pushed us both forward, so we fell, and he turned and ran away. I saw his flying robes, while Carlotta lay beside me, crying. Ah, yes. That would have been my father's initiation, his pledging to the East. Ah, yes, I understand it now."

"What happened?"

Almost calmly now, Charmian stared into the depth of time. "We lay there, frightened. And before we could get up, he came for us."

"He?"

"Lord Zapranoth. For his initiation, our father, had to give us to the Demon-Lord." Charmian's eyes now turned on Chup, but still her mind was in the past. "Lord Zapranoth reached for us, and I jumped to my feet and took Carlotta and pushed her in front of me, and I cried out: 'Take her! I am yours already. Already I serve the East'!" Charmian giggled, a pearly ripple of pure music, yet it made Chup draw back slightly. "I cried: 'Now take Carlotta as *my* pledging!' And Zapranoth stayed his hand, that had been reaching for us." Charmian's merriment faded suddenly. "And then he . . . laughed. That was a thing most horrible to hear. Then he put out his hand again, and stroked my h—"

Breaking off with a little shriek, Charmian clutched at the golden hair, that hung disheveled before her eyes, as if it were some alien creature settled on her head. Then she recovered herself somewhat, brushed back her hair and let it go. "Yes, Zapranoth stroked my hair. And later, when Elslood tried to make a love-charm from it—" She stopped.

"All Elslood's magic was confounded and reversed," Chup finished. "And he and every man who carried the charm was drawn to you by it. But never mind that now." He put out his hand slowly, not quite far enough to touch the gold that he had handled with rough carelessness not long ago. He said: "Do you suppose, that on that day—the Demon-Lord—might have left his *life* in this?"

The thought was no surprise to Charmian. "No, Chup. No. Hann examined my hair closely, when we were planning how best to use the charm, trying to find the source of its unusual power. Hann would have found a demon's life if it were there. We could have made the Demon-Lord our servant." She smiled. "No, Zapranoth would not have been fool enough to give his life into *my* keeping. He understood me far too well. When he had touched my hair, he said to me: 'Go freely from this cave, and serve the East. It has great need of such as you.' Yes. Now all the memories come back. My father was much amazed when I caught up with him. Much amazed to see me, and not entirely pleased. Oh, he looked back hopefully enough to see if my sister had also been released. She was the one he favored, truly cared for. But her the demon kept.

"And I think my father also was made to forget what happened here; at least he never spoke of it, or of Carlotta—Chup, what is it?"

He had got to his feet as if to face the enemy again, but he did not raise his weapon, only stared down fixedly at Charmian. Without taking his eyes from her he sheathed his sword and gripped her hands and pulled her to her feet. She twisted as if expecting another blow. But he only held her fast, demanding: "Tell me this. What was his aspect, when you saw him then?"

"Whose?"

"Zapranoth's." Chup's voice was not much louder than a whisper. "What did he look like then, what form did he take?" His eyes still bored relentlessly at her.

"Why, the form of a tall man, a giant, in dark armor. It matters little what form a demon takes. I knew him today, even at a distance, because the feeling he brought with him, the sickness, was the same—"

"Yes, yes!" He let her go. Caught by a powerful thought, he turned away, then turned right back. "You said that your sister was six years old, when the demon took her?"

"I don't know. About that, yes."

"And was she fair of face?"

"Some thought so. Yes."

"That could be changed—a small thing for the Demon-Lord," he murmured, staring past her into space. "What was the season of the year?"

"Chup, I—what does it matter now?"

"I tell you it does matter now!" He glared at Charmian again.

She closed her eyes and lined her perfect forehead with a frown. "It must have been six years ago. I think—no, it was in spring. Six and a half years ago, to this very season. I do not think I can calculate it any more closely—"

"Enough!" Chup slapped his hands together, rough triumph in his face and voice. "It must be so. It must be. The young fool said she came to them in springtime."

"What are you babbling of?" Charmain's temper edged her voice. "How can this help us now?"

"I don't know yet. What happened to your sister?"

Before Chup could finish the question there came a faint sound behind him and he had turned, sword drawn and ready. But the shape that dropped now to the narrow ledge was only a small brown furry creature, half the length of a sword from head to tail.

"Chupchupchupchup." Stretched as if in supplication on the ground, just outside of thrusting range, it opened a harmless-looking, flat-toothed mouth to make a noise between repeated gasps and hiccups. It took Chup a moment to understand this was a repetition of his name.

"Chupchupchup, the High Lord Draffut bids you come." The creature's speech was almost one long word, like something memorized and all but meaningless to the speaker. A beast as small as this one could not have much intelligence.

"I should come to the Lord Draffut?" Chup demanded. "Where? How?"

"Chup come, Chup come. Tell man Chup, now he is hunted, the High Lord Draffut bids him come to sanc-tu-ar-y. Haste and tell man Chupchupchup."

"How am I to come to him? Where? Show me the way."

As if to show Chup how, the little four-footed

animal spun around and bounded off, going up the side of the cliff again with ease, darting between rocks where a man could not easily have thrust an arm. Chup took one step, and then could only stare after it, hoping it might realize he could not follow.

He turned to Charmian. "How do you reckon that? If it's a trap, the bait's being kept safely out of reach, so distant I can't grab for it."

She shook her head, and seemed both envious and mystified. "It seems that you are genuinely offered sanctuary. I've heard that the small animals run the Beast-Lord's errands now and then. Does Draffut know you as an enemy of demons? That might account for it."

Before he could reply there came again the whispery slide of men trying to get at them from both sides. Perhaps they had seen the little messenger run past, and feared their prey was plotting an escape. As before, Chup smote the foe upon his right before the man could get his weapons up. This time the man on the left side was impeded by Charmian's falling at his feet. She had ducked for safety and lost her footing, and now she was clutching at her enemy's ankles while he was forced to concentrate on Chup. Much good his concentration did him with his feet immobilized; Chup's swordpoint tore him open and he toppled. Charmian let go his ankles quickly as his weight cleared the edge.

Chup spun back purposefully to the man he had struck down upon his right. It was the lieutenant of the Guards whom they had duped into letting them pass; he now had dropped his weapons and clung with blood-slippery, failing fingers to the rock. Chup cautiously pulled him in from the brink and cut his throat. Charmian watched, at first without understanding, as Chup continued cutting through the neck, gorily separating head from body.

When the collar of seamless-looking Old World metal was free, he wiped it clean on the lieutenant's uniform and held it up. With two motions of his foot he sent the headless body into the abyss.

By now she understood, or thought she did. Anger was in her voice, perhaps from envy or from fear of being left alone. "You are a fool. The valkyrie will take no unhurt man to the Lord Draffut. And none who does not wear the collar properly around his neck."

"You are not entirely right in that, my lady. I have talked with the soldiers. The valkyries *will* take a man whose collar is off. Provided he is so wounded that his head is severed from his trunk."

Now her face showed that she fully understood his plan. Her anger grew. "Not every dead man is brought to Lord Draffut's domain in time to be restored, nor heals properly."

"Nor has a personal invitation from the High Lord Draffut. Listen, lady, I think you will not be worse off if I go. If more soldiers scramble down here, you may do as well with your eyelashes and sweet voice as I would with a sword. As things stand now, you can't get out of here."

That was true; now she was listening.

He pressed on. "Your situation may be greatly helped if I can go. What I was saying when the animal came is more important now than ever. What happened to your sister?"

"The Lord of Demons took her, as I said. Devoured her, I suppose."

"You *saw* the tall black man do that?"

"I . . . no. He laid his hand upon her, and her screams were quieted. I did not linger to see more."

With a quick movement Chup reversed his sword, and held the pommel of it out to Charmian. "Take this."

She stood in hesitation.

Chup said: "If the Beast-Lord hates demons, as you say, I had better go to him, and quickly."

"Why?"

"To tell him where to find the life of Zapranoth. Now take this and cut off my head."

Holding out the sword and waiting, Chup felt content. True, she might murder him good, or his plan might fail for other reasons. But since he had turned his back on Som and on the East, he felt like his own man again, and that feeling was enough; perhaps it was all that a man like him should try to get from life.

He fought on now to win, to live, because that was his nature. But he was tired, and saw no future beyond this battle. Death in itself had never been a terror for him. If it came now—well, he was tired. Half a year of paralytic near-death he had endured, out of sheer pride, unwillingness to give in. Then, when as if by miracle, his strength and freedom had been returned to him, he had come near throwing them away again, to serve the East—and why? What power or treasure could they offer that was worth the price they asked?

"Strike off my head," he said to Charmian. "A valkyrie must be coming for this collar by now; there'd be one already here if they weren't having a busy day."

She was still hesitating, fearing, hoping, thinking, desperately deciding what course was best for her own welfare. She reached out and took the sword, then asked him: "Where is the demon's life concealed?"

"Lady, I would not trust you with my beheading, save that you must see how it is in your own interest for me to reach Draffut with what I know. If we can kill or threaten Zapranoth, and tip the battle to the West, then you may sit here safely until Som is no longer dangerous. Unless, of course, *you* would rather bear the message; in which case I must cut off your—no. I thought not."

He turned and knelt down slowly, face toward the cliff. Charmian was at his right, holding the long blade point down on the ground. He said: "Now, about this little surgery I need . . . I suppose a single stroke would be too much to ask for. But more than two or three should not be needed, the blade is heavy and quite sharp." Without turning to see her face, he added: "You are most beautiful, and most desirable by far, of all the women I have ever known."

From the corner of his eye he saw Charmian losing her hesitation, gathering resolve, straightening her thin wrists in a tight two-handed grip to lift the weapon's weight. Chup studied the details of the rock wall straight before him.

He had knelt down facing this way so that his head would not roll over—

Enough of that. He was Chup. He would not even close his eyes.

On its way, the sword sang thinly. His muscles cried for the signal to roll away, his nerves screamed that there was still time to dodge. His ruling mind held his neck stretched and motionless.

IX

Before the Citadel

———————◆•◆•◆———————

Out near the middle of the tableland that divided the forces of the East and West, in a part of the rough plateau that was shattered and split into a dozen peninsulas divided by abyssal crevices, the High Lord Zapranoth came bursting up into the morning air like some foul pall of smoke, from a huge chimney-opening in the ground. Rolf, turning from his work of grappling down great gasbags, looked up at Zapranoth and saw that which made him squint his eyes half shut and turn away—though he could not have said what it was about the smoke that was so terrible. Looking around him, he could see that only Gray, and Loford who now stood beside his brother, were able to face the demon with their heads raised and eyes wide open. They were standing in the rear of the invaders' little line, near Rolf and the balloons. The smoky image of the technology-djinn was fluttering and darting to and fro above the gasbags, like some frantic bird confined in an invisible cage.

Now Gray raised both his arms. Before the face of Zapranoth there appeared a haze or reflection of light gray, a screen as insubstantial as a rainbow, but as persistent. It stood steadily before the demon as he drifted gently nearer. Now it was possible for the soldiers of the West to look toward him—and toward the citadel, through whose open gate the Guard and its auxiliaries were pouring out, quick-march. Arrows began to fly both ways across the field. When the defenders of the citadel had finished a quick and practiced deployment in four ranks, Rolf estimated there might be nearly a thousand of them. He was too busy to give much time to pondering the odds, for the last balloons were landing now and he and his assistants had all they could do with work and dodging arrows. Each wore on his left arm a light shield woven of green limber branches; such shields were thought capable of squeezing and stopping piercing shafts that could bite through a coat of mail.

"Sound the trumpet once more!" Thomas now ordered with a shout. The Northman with the horn, his head now bandaged, turned back to face the pass—its thread of road still empty—and once more blasted out the signal.

This time there came an answering horn, though it sounded dishearteningly far away.

"There is our army coming, friends!" Thomas shouted in a great voice. "Let's see if we can do the job before they get here!"

As if the distant horn had been a signal for them too, the Guard swayed now in formation to the shouting of its officers, and as one man stepped forward to attack. At a range of a hundred and fifty meters there came from their rear ranks a volley of arrows.

Rolf and those around him, finished at last with tying down balloons, took up their weapons and moved into their places for the fight. Some, holding shields, raised them to protect Gray and Loford. The two wizards still were standing motionless, and gazing steadfastly upon the ominous but also nearly motionless bulk of Zapranoth, high in the air above the middle of the field. Loford was swaying slightly on his feet; there was no other overt sign as yet of the struggle of invisible powers that had been joined.

The horn from down below, within the pass, now sounded once more, noticeably closer; and again as if its signal had been meant for them, the Guard of Som the Dead began to run and came on in a yelling charge.

The broken ground delayed them unequally, so that their lines were bent. Rolf, with bow in hand and arrows laid out before him on the ground, knelt in the middle of a line of archers. He took little time to aim, but loosed into the oncoming swarm of men in black, nocked and drew and loosed again. The air was thick with dust and missiles, and his targets moved confusingly, so it was difficult to tell what damage his own shots were doing. Certainly the ranks of black were thinning as they came. A steady droning sprang up in the air above, as the valkyries whirred industriously, in madly methodical calm they dipped into the fury of the fight below to lift the fallen warriors of Som and take them to the high place of Lord Draffut. Some machines flew through the image of the Demon-Lord, with no awareness shown on either side. It was as if each were unreal to the other, and only humans must know and deal with both.

There was no thought of saving arrows; if this attack was not stopped there would be no need to worry about the next. The man next to Rolf went down, killed by a flung stone. Others were falling in the Western ranks, but those thin lines did not pull back. Behind them was the cliff edge, or defeat and death retreating down the pass. They braced themselves instead, and readied pike and battle-axe and sword.

By now some of the enemy were come so close to Rolf that he could hear them gasping as they ran, and see the hair on hands that lifted swords to strike. Rolf threw his bow behind him and rose up in a crouch, shield on arm and sword in hand.

An Eastern officer, marked by the plume upon his helmet, came running past in front of Rolf, with great arm-wavings urging his men on. Rolf leaped forward to get in striking range, but was checked by another Guardsman charging at him. This foe was running blindly, already berserk with battle, his eyes seemed to look unseeing through Rolf even as he swung a mace. Rolf dodged back, then stepped in—not as neatly as the nimblest warriors could, but well enough to avoid this weapon, only half-controllable. Rolf cut his sword into the Guards-man's running legs, felt shin bones splinter, saw the man go plowing forward on his face.

One of the Northmen on Rolf's left started his own countercharge, striding into the foe, making a de-sert round him with a great two-handed blade. Those of the enemy who did not fall back before this giant tried to spread around him and get at him from the sides. Rolf hung back a step until he had outflanked the liveliest of these flankers, then lunged in for the kill. The man was more than half armored, but Rolf's sword point found a soft place in between the hipbone and the ribs. As that man fell, another came, but this one straight at Rolf. This new opponent was the better swordsman, but Rolf would not yield an inch. He warded one stroke after another, somehow, until the Northman's long sword on its backswing wounded his enemy from behind. The odds were more than evened, and the foe went staggering back until the ranks of black had hidden him.

Then all at once there were no more of the enemy menacing, but only the retreating horde of their black backs.

"What? What is it?" Rolf demanded. Mewick had come from somewhere and had taken him by the arm.

"—bind it up," Mewick was saying.

"What?" All the world, for Rolf, was still quivering with the shock of battle. He could not feel nor hear nor think of anything else.

"You are hurt. See, here. Not bad, but we must bind it up."

"Ah." Looking down, Rolf saw a small gash on the upper part of his left arm. He could not feel the slightest pain. His shield woven of green limber withes, that had been on his left arm, was all but gone now, hacked to bits. He could not recall now which of his enemies had dealt these blows, nor how he had avoided being killed by them.

The soldiers on both sides were reforming lines, just out of easy arrow range, and binding wounds. And while the valkyries went droning on, without rest or hesitation, some men of the West hurried, at Thomas' orders, to behead the enemy who had fallen among them, gather their metal collars and throw them over the cliff. This was the only way they had discovered to prevent their foemen's restoration. No blow from any weapon that a man could wield could stay a valkyrie from gathering up a fallen man; the Westerners learned this quickly, and then saved their breath and effort and the edges of their blades. They only grumbled and dodged the vicious, blurring rotors that smashed the pikemen's weapons down and broke their fingers when they tried to interfere.

One of Mewick's countrymen was calling: "Look —our boys in sight now, at the bottom of the pass. Look!"

Men turned and gathered, looking down the pass. Rolf joined them, his arm now bandaged and his mind a little clearer. He felt no great emotion at the sight of reinforcements coming.

"They're running now that they're in sight," said someone. "But it seems they've been all day about it."

"Only a few in sight yet, with light weapons. The mass of 'em are still far down."

There was short time to celebrate, even had there been greater inclination. The Guard was fast reforming. Their ranks were still impressively superior in size to those of the invaders, whose small force seemed to Rolf's eye to have been drastically diminished. He started to count how many were still on their feet, and then decided he would rather not.

Now once again the Demon-Lord was drifting slowly closer, his image rolling like a troubled cloud. The screen of protective magic that Gray had thrown up before Zapranoth yielded to the demon's pressure but stayed squarely in his path.

Neither Loford nor Gray had ducked or dodged or moved a hand to save themselves as yet. Around them tall protective shields had been held up, by the minor wizards who had abandoned any thought of dueling Zapranoth themselves. More than one had fallen, by stone or arrow, of these men protecting Gray and Loford. Neither one of the two strong wizards had been struck by any material weapon, but anyone looking at their faces now might think that both were wounded.

A darkness like the dying of the sun fell round the two tall magicians now. It was the shadow cast by Zapranoth as he loomed nearer. And now, for the first time on this field, his voice came booming forth: "Are these the wizards of the West who seek to murder me? Ho, Gray, where is my life? Will you pull it out now from your little satchel?" Still the thin gray screen before him held, but now it flared and flickered raggedly, and still he slowly pressed it back.

"Come now," boomed Zapranoth, "favor me with an answer, mighty magician. Admit me to your august company. Let me speak to you. Let me touch you, if only timidly."

At that Loford gave a weak cry and toppled, senseless, and would have struck the ground head-long if some standing near him had not caught him first.

Now Gray stood alone against the pressure of the dark shape above. He cried out too, and swayed, but did not fall. Instead he straightened himself with some reserve of inner strength, and with his arms flung wide set his fingers moving in a pattern as intricate as that a musician makes upon a keyboard. There sprang up gusts of wind as sudden and violent as the firing of catapults, so men who stood near Gray were thrown to the ground, and dust and pebbles were blasted into the air, in savage streams that crisscrossed through the heart of Zapranoth before they lost velocity and fell in a rain of dirt into the citadel three hundred meters distant.

The image of the demon did not waver in the least. But these howling shafts of wind were only the forerunners, the scouts and skirmishers, of the tremendous power that Gray in his extremity had set in motion; Rolf saw this, glancing behind him over the cliff edge to the west. There where the sky some moments earlier had been azure and calm, there now advanced a line of clouds, roiling and galloping at a pace far faster than a bird could fly. These clouds, confined to a thin flat plane a little above the level of the citadel, converged like charging cavalry upon the waiting, looming bulk of Zapranoth.

An air-elemental, thought Rolf, with awe and fear and hope commingled; he would have shouted it aloud, but no one could have heard him through the screaming wind.

The violence of that wind was concentrated at the level of the Demon-Lord, well above the field where humans walked and fought. Men found that they could stand and swing their weapons though they staggered with the heavier gusts. And now the Guard came charging on again. Rolf put on his arm a shield taken from a fallen Easterner, gripped his sword hard, and waited in the line. While over their heads a torrent of air and cloud-forms thundered from the west to beat like surf upon the image of the demon, men lowered their eyes and worked to injure one another with their blades, like ants at war on some tumultuous wave-pounded beach.

The earlier fight had seemed to Rolf quite short. This one was endless, and several times he despaired of coming through alive. Mewick, howling like the wind, fought this time on Rolf's right hand, and saved him more than once. Somehow he was not even wounded in this attack, which failed as the first one had.

While the warriors fought, the violence of the wind gradually abated; and even as the black-clad host fell back once more in dissarray, the weightless bulk of Zapranoth again came pressing forward.

"Gray!" Thomas, stumbling on a wounded leg, came forcing his way through to the wizard's side. "Hang on, our men are coming!" Even now the first gasping and exhausted troops of the climbing Western army were nearing the top of the pass; the bulk of that army, on its thousands of laboring legs, was now in sight though far below.

Gray slowly, with the movement of an old, old man, turned his head to Thomas. In Gray's face, that seemed to be aging by the moment, there was at first no hint of understanding.

Thomas raised his voice. "You, and you, support him on his feet. Gray, do not fail us now. What can we do?"

The answer came feebly, as from the lips of a dying man: "You had better win with the sword, and quickly. I will hold the demon off till my last breath . . . that is not far away."

Thomas looked round to see that the vanguard of his main army was just arriving at the top of the pass, brave men too exhausted for the moment by their running climb to do anything but sit and gasp for air, and squint up doubtfully at the looming shape of Zapranoth. The winds had driven the demon some distance from the field; whether they had inflicted pain or injury upon him no one could tell save Gray, perhaps. Of the screen of white magic Gray had earlier thrown up, there were only traces left, flickering and flaring like the last flames of a dying fire.

Rolf found it was no longer bearable to look straight at the Demon-Lord.

"One man run down," Thomas was ordering, pointing down the pass to the approaching reinforcements. "Tell any with the least skill in magic to push on before the other, and hurry!" He turned his helmet's T-shaped opening toward Rolf. "Ready the balloons for the attack upon the citadel itself! We must not sit here waiting for the demon to set the course of battle."

Rolf sheathed his sword and turned and ran shouting to rally his crew to the balloons. At his direction men put down weapons, eased off armor, took up tools and ropes. The technology-djinn, still constrained by the spells that Gray had put upon it, obeyed Rolf's orders when he called them out.

When he could look up from his work again, Rolf saw that the Guard of Som had been reformed once more on the plain. The ranks of black were not greatly smaller than they had been at the start of the day's carnage; Guard replacements were trotting out from the citadel wearing torn and bloodstained garments in which they had already been slain once today. But the Guard had missed its chance to push the stubborn West from its small foothold on the height; the trickle of reinforcement up the pass had thickened steadily. Soon it would become a flow of hundreds and of thousands.

There were wizards of diverse but minor skills ascending with the army; each of these as he arrived was hurried to the side of Gray, who still was conscious, though standing only with the help of strong men on each side. But one by one these lesser magicians fell away, nearly as fast as they arrived and sought to relieve Gray of some part of the invisible power of Zapranoth. Some crumpled soundlessly. Some leaped and fell, groaning as if struck by arrows. One man tore with his nails at his flesh, screamed wildly, and before he could be stopped, leaped from the precipice.

Rolf took it all in with a glance. "We are ready!" he shouted to Thomas.

"Then fill your baskets with good men, and fly! We will be with you there."

Most of the survivors of the original assault force, being the type of men they were, had already boarded for the next attack. The wind seemed right. But Zapranoth was coming, rushing now toward them like a toppling wall. Rolf, in the act of boarding his balloon, looked up and cried out at the sight. With the majesty and darkness of a thundercloud great Zapranoth now passed above them; it was as if the skirts of his robe spilled madness and dragged lightning. Two of the balloons burst thunderously, even as the djinn in its invisible cage became a blur of terror. Above the djinn there lowered a drifting fringe of cloud, that in the winking of an eye became a closing pair of massive jaws. With the devouring of the djinn, Gray cried out in despair and pain, and his head rolled loosely on his neck.

Men were running, falling, waving weapons in the air. In the confusion Rolf lost sight of Thomas, who had not yet given the last order to cast off. But there was no doubt what must be done; the balloons were ready, a little wind still held. Even without the djinn they could rise up and drop again upon the citadel.

"Cast off!" Rolf shouted left and right; ropes were let go, and his flotilla rose and flew. The demon that had just passed by now turned, but did not strike at the balloons; perhaps Gray was not yet wholly overcome. As the craft passed over the formation of the Guard, stones and arrows made a thick buzzing swarm around them. Shafts pierced every gasbag, though the padded baskets shielded the men inside. But their flight was not intended to be far.

Lowering again, they reached the citadel's low wall, and for the most part cleared it. Along the top of the wall, behind its parapet, one lean man in black came running toward the invaders as if to fight them all, while others ran away—by his behavior Rolf knew Som the Dead. But in another moment Som was left behind.

Inside the walls, the silent flyers skimmed above a different world, one that was still ordered, peaceful, pleasant to the eye. Trees, hedges, and the rooftops of low sprawling buildings skimmed the basket bottoms. There fled before them women in rich silks and furs, and a few servants in drab dress.

Only one person besides Som remained to watch them boldly. One young servant girl who had mounted a low roof gazed at the balloons, and past them at the battle. Rolf passed near enough to get a good look at her face.

It was his sister Lisa.

X

Lake of Life

There was a steady swell of sound, a moaning endless tone so long prolonged in his strange loneliness that Chup could not imagine or remember when he had begun to hear it; and this odd swelling was a light as well, of which he could not remember his first sight, so bright he did not need his eyes to see it, but not too bright for eyes in spite of that.

And it was a touch, a pressure, of an intensity to make it unendurable if it had been felt in one place or even many, but it bore in all directions on every fiber, inward and outward, so all the infinity of opposing pressures balanced and there was no pain. Chup lived encompassed in this swelling thing like a fish within the sea, immersed and saturated and supported by inexhaustible sound, pressure, light, odor, taste, heat of fire and cold of ice, all balanced to a point of nothingness and adding up to everything.

So he lived, without remembering how he had come to be so living, remembering only the soft and singing promise of the sword. He did not waken, for he had not slept. Then: I am Chup, he thought. This is what the beheaded see.

What had jogged him into thinking was the feel of someone prosaically pulling on his hair. He did not open his eyes now, for they were already open. He could see light and soft pleasant colors, flowing downward. Up he rose, pulled by his hair, until he broke with a slow splash of glory back into the world of air, in which his senses once more functioned separately.

He was in a cave. He could not at once be certain of its size, but he thought it was enormous. The overhead curve of its roof was too smoothly rounded to be natural. The upper part of the cave was filled with light, though its rounded sides and top were dark; the lower part, up to what was perhaps the middle, was filled with the glowing fluid from which Chup had just been lifted, an enclosed lake of restless energy. Chup knew now that he had reached his goal, what he had heard the soldiers call the Lake of Life.

Like some gigantic bear reared on two legs, immersed to his middle in the lake, there stood the shaggy figure of a beast. His fur was radiant, of many colors or of none, as if of the same substance as the lake. Chup could not see the creature's face as yet, because he could not turn or lift his head. Chup's head swung like a pendulum, neckless and bodiless, from what must be this great beast's grip on his long hair.

He could, however, move his eyes. Where his body should have been below his chin there was nothing to be seen except receding strings of droplets, not gore, but drops of multicolored glory from the lake. Falling dripping from his neck stump, out of sight beneath his chin, the droplets splashed and merged into the glowing lake whence they had come. Chup understood now that he, his head, had been immersed and saturated in the lake, and that had been enough to restore life, with no least sense of shock or pain.

The grip upon his hair now turned his pendulum-head around, and now he saw the High Lord Draffut's face. It was a countenance of enormous ugliness and power, more beast than human certainly, but gentle in repose. And now Chup saw that in his other hand the Beast-Lord held like a doll

the nude and headless body of a man. Like a child
washing a doll he held the body down, continually
dipping and washing it in the Lake of Life. With the
splashing and the motion the brilliance of the liquid
intensified into soft explosions of color, modulating
in waves of light the steady gentle lumination of the
air inside the cave.

And now, in his enormous shaggy hand, very like a
human hand in shape but far more powerful and
beautiful, the High Lord Draffut raised the headless
thing and like a craftsman turned it for his own
inspection. Like that of one newborn, or newly slain,
the muscular body writhed and floundered uncon-
trolled. On its skin Chup could count his old scars,
like a history of his life. He marked the jaggedness of
the neck stump, where Charmian had hacked and
sliced unskillfully. From its severed veins the elixir
of the lake came pumping out like blood, and tinged
with blood.

The hand that held Chup's head up by its hair
now shifted its grip slightly. Turning his eyes down
once again, he beheld his own headless, living body
being brought up close beneath his head. Its hands
grasped clumsily, like a baby's, at Draffut's fur when
they could feel it. Closer the raw neck stump came,
till Chup could hear the fountaining of its blood
vessels. And closer yet, until there came a pressure
underneath his chin —

His head had not been breathing, nor felt any
need to breathe; now there came a choking feeling,
but it entailed no pain. It ended as the first rush of
lung-drawn air caught coldly in his mouth and
throat. Then with a sharp tingle came the feelings of
his body, awareness of his fingers clutched in fur, of
his feet kicking in the air, of the gentle pressure of
the great hand closed around his ribs.

That hand now bore him down, to immerse him
completely in the lake once more. Once he was
below the surface, his breathing stopped again, not
by any choking or impediment but simply because it

was not needed there. A man plunged into clearest, purest water would not call for a cup of muddy scum to drink; so it was that his lungs made no demand for air. Then in two hands Chup was lifted out, to be held high before an ugly, gentle face that watched him steadily.

"I came—" Chup began to speak with a shout, before he realized there was no need for loudness. The lake gave the impression of filling all the cave with waterfall-voices, as sweet as demons' noise was foul, but yet in fact a whisper might be heard.

"I came as quickly as I could, Lord Draffut," he said more normally. "I thank you for my life."

"You are welcome to what help I have to give. It is long since any thanked me for it." The voice of Draffut, deep and deliberate, was fit for a giant. His hands turned Chup like a naked babe undergoing a midwife's last inspection. Then Draffut set him, still dripping with the lake, upon a ledge that—Chup now saw—ran all the way around the cavern. This ledge, and the huge cave's walls and curving roof, were of some substance dark and solid as the goblet in which the demon had brought him his healing draught long days ago. The ledge was at a level but little higher than the surface of the lake. Seeing at a distance was difficult in the cavern's glowing air, but at its farthest point from Chup the ledge seemed wider, like a beach, and there were other figures moving on it, perhaps of other beasts who tended other men.

The Beast-Lord said: "I cannot command the valkyries, or I would have sent them for you. If I could choose what men I help, I would help first those who fight against the demons."

Chup opened his mouth to answer. But now that he was no longer bathed in the fluid of life, a great weakness came over him, and he could only lean back against the wall and feebly nod.

"Rest," said Draffut. "You will grow stronger quickly, here. Then we will talk. I would give all men sanctuary, and heal them, but I cannot . . . I sent for you because you are the first man in the Black Mountains in many years who has cared for a fellow creature's suffering. A small beast brought me the news that you had saved it from a demon."

For a moment Chup could not remember, but then it came to him: in the cavern of Som's treasure hoard. Still he was too feeble to do more than nod.

He tried again to study the figures moving in the cavern's farthest reaches, but could not see them clearly, so vibrant was the air with light and life. The ledge Chup rested on was of a dull and utter black, but covered tightly with a film as thin and bright as sunlight, a glowing, transparent skin formed of the fluid of the lake. The film was never still. At one spot there would begin a thickening in the film, a thickening that swelled and pulsed, rose up and broke away, becoming a living separation that went winging like a butterfly. And from some other place there would spring a similar fragment, perhaps bigger than the first, big enough to be a bird, flying up and sagging as its wings melted, but not dying or collapsing, only putting out new wings of some different and more complex shape and flying on to collide in the singing, luminous air with the butterfly, the two of them clinging together and trembling, seeming on the verge of growing into something still bigger and more wonderful; but then diving deliberately together and melting back into the gracefully swirling body of the lake, with their plunge splashing up droplets that fell again into the patterned film that glided shining and without ceasing over the black substance of the ledge.

Feeling some returning strength, Chup raised one hand to touch his neck. Running his fingers all the way around, he followed the scar, thin, jagged, and painless, of his death wound. Once more he tried to talk.

"Lord Draffut, is the battle over?"

Draffut turned his head toward the far end of the

Lake. "My machines are still working without pause. The battle goes on. From what I have heard from beasts and men, the foul demon is likely to prevail, though if the issue were left to swords alone, the West would win."

"Then there is little time for us to act." Chup tried to rise, but felt no stronger than the splashing butterflies of light.

"Your healing is not finished. Wait, you soon will be strong enough to stand. What do you mean, we must act?"

"We must act against the one you call 'foul demon'—if you are as much the demons' enemy as you claim, and I have heard."

Draffut lifted his great forearms high, then let them down, like falling trees, with a huge splash. "Demons! They are the only living things that I would kill, if I could. They devour men's lives, and waste their bodies. For no need of their own, but out of sheer malignity, they steal the healing fluid from my lake, and taunt me when I rage and cannot come to grips with them."

Chup was now able to sit straighter on the ledge, and his voice had grown stronger. "You would kill Zapranoth?"

"Him soonest of them all! Of all the demons that I know, he has done human beings the greatest harm."

"I know where he has hidden his life."

All was silent, except for the sweet seashell roaring of the lake. Draffut, standing absolutely still, looked down steadily at Chup for so long that Chup began to wonder if a trance had come upon him.

Then Draffut spoke at last. "Here in the citadel? Where we can reach it?"

"Here in the citadel he hid it, where he could keep his eye upon it every day. Where we can reach it if we are strong and fierce enough."

The Beast-Lord's hands, knotted into barrel-sized fists, rose dripping from the lake. "Fierce? I can be fierce enough for anything, against obstacles that do not live, or against demons, or even against beasts if there is need. I cannot injure men. Not even—when it must be done."

"I can, and will again." With a great effort Chup rose up, swaying, to his feet. "Som and his demon-loving crew . . . as soon as I can hold a sword again. Lord Draffut, the human Lords of the East are more like demons than like men." Lifting a weak arm, Chup pointed to the distant beachlike place, where people were being cared for by tall inhuman figures. "Who are those?"

"Those? My machines. At least they were machines, when I was young. We all have changed since then, working in this cave, in constant contact with the Lake of Life. Now they are alive."

Chup had no time for marveling at that. "I mean those being healed. If you would fight the demons, fight the men who help them. Turn against the East. Order your machines, beasts, whatever they are, to stop healing Som's troops now."

At that, Lord Draffut's eyes blazed down upon him. "I have never seen Som, let alone acknowledged him as lord, and I care nothing for him. Men come and go around my lake, and use it. I remain. Long before there was an East or West, I lived. From the days of the Old World I have healed human wounds. Weapons were different then, but wounds were much the same, and men change not at all—though to me they then were gods."

Were what? Chup wondered, fleetingly; he had not heard that word before.

Draffut spoke on, as if relieving himself of thoughts and words too long pent up. "I was not in the Old World as you see me now. Then I could not think. I was much smaller, and ran behind human beings on four legs. But I could love them, and I did, and I must love them still. Turn against the East, you say? I am no part of that abomination! I was here before Som came—long before—and I mean to be here when he has gone. I walked here when the healing lake was made, by men who thought their war would be the last. When they went mad and ran away, I was locked in, with the machines. I—grew. And when new tribes of humanity came, I was ready to lend them the collars, and the valkyries' help, that they might be healed when they fought. And— after them—came others—''

The High Lord Draffut slowed his angry speech. ''Enough of that. Where is the life of Zapranoth?''

Chup told him, things that he had heard and seen, and how the pieces seemed to fall together. The telling was quickly finished, but Chup was standing straight before he'd finished; he felt his strength increasing by the moment. ''The girl's name is the same, you see. Lisa. Though I would wager that her face and memory have been changed. And she has been here just half a year.''

Draffut pondered but a moment more. ''Then come, Lord Chup, and I will give you arms. If there are men I cannot frighten from our path, then you will fight them. If what you say is true, no other obstacle can keep me from the life of Zapranoth. Come! Swim!'' And Draffut turned and swam away, cleaving the lake with stretching overhand strokes. Chup dove in and followed, faster than he had ever splashed through water.

XI

Knife of Fire

———◆◆◆———

Rolf's balloon skimmed lower, dragged against tall shrubbery, and scraped free, but then continued sinking. In the quiet he could hear the gas escaping from a dozen arrow punctures in the bag. Mewick pointed silently at the next hedge ahead of them; this one they would not clear.

Rolf swung up to the basket's rim, and leaped in the instant before they struck the hedge. He hit the ground with sword already drawn — but there were no opponents yet in sight.

In all directions, other balloons were coming down, seeding armed desperate fighters throughout the inner courts and buildings of Som's citadel. But some balloons had missed the walls, or were still going up. Lacking the djinn's help, or guiding ropes to follow, there was no pattern in the landing. Mewick was to assume leadership of the five man squad in Rolf's balloon, once they had landed. But Mewick, like the rest, now stood perplexed for a moment beside the hedge; it was hard to see which was the best way to move to join up most effectively with other elements of the assaulting force. And from this garden they could see no vulnerable target where Som might be hurt with a quick attack.

Only Rolf had glimpsed a goal, and he turned toward it when it seemed as likely a direction to take as any other. He ran toward the place where he had seen his sister, Mewick and the others pounding after him, across empty lawns and over deserted terraces.

The girl was still on the roof. Her face was turned away, toward the battlefield, where like the smoke of burning villages the Demon-Lord hung in the air.

"Lisa!"

She looked round when he shouted, and he knew he had not been mistaken. But there was no recognition in her eyes when they met his, only confusion and alarm.

Rolf started toward her, but then stopped as a squad of men in black appeared, coming in single file round the corner of the building where she was.

He called out once more: "Lisa, try to come this way!" But there was no way for her to manage that right now. The Eastern squad was coming on to block the way. They were only auxiliaries, without the collars of the Guard, and armed with a varied selection of old weapons, but they were eight to face Rolf and his four companions. The eight soon proved to lack the willingness for battle of the five; one of their number they left behind, bleeding his life out in a flowerbed, and others, fleeing, clutched at wounds and yelled and left red trails.

Rolf tried to get another look at Lisa on her roof. But there was no time. Beyond a tall hedge and a wall of masonry, some thirty meters distant, a huge collapsing gasbag showed where another Western squad had landed. These now seemed heavily beset, to judge by the shouts and noises there. Another force in black, ten or twelve men maybe, could be glimpsed through hedges as they hurried in that direction.

Drops of gore flew from Mewick's hatchet as he motioned for a charge. "That way!" And they were off.

The shortest route to this new fight, lay over a decorative stone wall, head high. Rolf sheathed his sword to hurl himself up at full speed and with two hands free to grab. He drew again even as he lunged onward from his crouch atop the wall, and as he leaped struck downward with full force, to kill a

Guardsman from behind. They were in a walled-in
garden, with more than a score of men contending
in a wild melee. Rolf landed awkwardly, off balance,
but bounced up into a crouch at once, just in time to
parry a hard blow that nearly knocked his sword
away.

Above the garden the huge gasbag, draped with its
plastic mail, was steadily collapsing, threatening to
make a temporary peace by smothering the fight.
But yet there was room to wield weapons. The five
beleaguered crewmen of this balloon welcomed
with shouts the arrival of Mewick and his squad,
and doubled their own strokes. But this time the
enemy were Guardsmen, and more numerous than
the squad of auxiliaries had been.

The fight was savage and protracted. The West
could gain no advantage until the crew of a third
balloon had managed to reach the scene, and fell
upon the Guardsmen's flank. When at last the Guard
retreated, there were but nine men of the West still
on their feet, and several of these were weak with
wounds. Rolf, bearing only the one light wound suf-
fered earlier, helped others with their bandages. He
then began to hack off fallen Guardsmen's heads,
but Mewick stopped him.

"We must move on, and find some heart or brain
within this citadel where we can strike; let dead
men be."

One of the Northmen had got up into a tree to look
around. "More of our fellows over there! Let's link
with them!"

Over the wall again they went, to where another
dozen or fifteen Westerners had joined together,
and were setting fires. Mewick was quick to argue
with the leader of these men that what they were
doing had little purpose, that some vital target must
be found. To make his point he gestured toward the
battlefield outside the citadel. There the High Lord
Zapranoth remained immobile above the Western

force; and what the demon might be doing to the men who swarmed like ants beneath his feet was not something that Rolf cared to think about.

But the leader of the vandalizing crew, gestured to the clouds of smoke his men were causing to go up; these, he shouted, were bound to have an effect when they were seen.

And he was right. A hundred black-clad soldiers or more, diverted from the fight outside, came pouring back into the citadel. Som dared not let his fortress and its contents fall.

This Eastern counterattack came with a volley of arrows, then a charge. Rolf once more caught sight of Som himself, entering the fight in person in defense of what might be his own sprawling manor. The Lord of the Black Mountains, gaunt and hollow-eyed, wearing no shield or armor, shouting orders, came striding at the head of his own troops, swinging a two-handed sword. A Western crossbowman atop a wall let fly a bolt at Som. Rolf saw the missile blur halfway to its black-clad target, spin neatly in midair, then fly back with the same speed it had been fired. It tore a hole clear through the bowman's throat.

After that, there were few weapons raised at Som, though he ran straight at the Western line. Hack and thrust as he might, hoping to provoke a counter, those of the West who came within his reach restricted themselves to parrying and dodging his blows. Fortunately he was no great swordsman, and could do little damage to such a line as faced him now, shields at the ready. Once his sword was knocked out of his hands. He grabbed it up again, his face a mask of rage, and leaped once more to the attack. This time the Western line divided just in front of him; Mewick had quickly hatched a scheme to cut off Som and capture him, by a ring of shields pressed round him till he could be immobilized and disarmed. But the opening appeared too neatly be-

fore Som, or perhaps some magic warned him; he
fell back into the shelter of his own ranks, and
thenceforward was content to let them do his fighting. They came on sturdily enough.

Once more, for a time, the fighting was without
letup. Then there came another small body of Western troops, fighting their way into the mass, better-
ing the odds just when it seemed they were about to
worsen too severely. The forces separated briefly,
the West dragging back their wounded where they
had the chance. Rolf, looking again for Lisa, saw that
she had remained at her vantage point on the roof.
Perhaps she felt safer up there. Looking beyond her,
he saw the sign of defeat still in the sky — the brooding shape of Zapranoth.

One of the party who had just joined them had
thrown himself down, exhausted, and was answering questions about the progress of the battle outside. Rolf realized that this man and his group had
just come from there, had somehow managed to
fight their way over the citadel's wall or through its
gate.

"—but it does not go well. The old man with-
stands the demon still, how I do not know. Surely he
cannot live much longer. Then Zapranoth will have
us all. Already half our army has gone mad. They
throw away their weapons, chew on rocks . . . still
we have numbers on our side, and we might win, if it
were not for Zapranoth. None can withstand the
demon. None . . ."

His voice fell silent. The men around were looking
at him no longer, but up toward the mountain.

Rolf craned his neck. There, on the high, barren,
unclimbable slope, amid the doors where valkyries
shuttled in and out, a new door had been opened. It
looked as if an outer layer of rock had been cracked
away as the door, of heavy dull black stuff, had been
swung out. Framed in the opening, there stood what
seemed to be the figure of a man, but having a

beast's head, and garbed in fur as radiant as fire. From inside the mountain, behind this figure, there streamed out a coruscating light that made Rolf think of molten metal.

And now he saw that the figure could not be human, for there was a real man beside him; smaller than an infant by comparison, but armed with a bright needle of a sword, and clothed in black like some lord of the East.

"Lord Draffut!" cried out someone in the Eastern force.

"Who will heal us if he should fall?" another called.

Other shouts of astonishment came from the Guard. They, like their enemies facing them, were lowering their weapons momentarily and looking up to marvel.

Lord Draffut bent, picked up the man beside him in one hand, and held him cradled in one arm. Then striding down the slope Lord Draffut came, walking boldly on two legs where it seemed no man could have climbed. It was as if he walked in snow or gravel, instead of solid stone; for at his touch, rock melted, not with heat but as if quickening briefly into crawling life, to quiet again when he had passed.

Though the Lord Draffut carried no weapon but one armed man, his attitude and pace were those of one who came on eagerly to enter battle. Yet from the ranks of the East there came no cheers. All men still watched in blank surprise, half of them with weapons dragging in the dirt. Som himself was peering up as if he could not credit what was happening before his eyes.

Draffut's great strides quickly brought him close to the citadel. Then he had entered it, sliding down the last near-vertical face of rock that served as its rear wall. Behind him stretched a line of tracks left in the dead solidity of the mountain.

The men of the West who were inside the citadel contracted their defensive line now, and gripped their weapons tightly; there was no place for them to run. Then gradually they understood that Draffut and his rider were not coming straight toward them—not quite. The tiny-looking man in black raised his bare sword and pointed, and the striding lord he rode accomodatingly made a slight correction in his course. The rider's black garments, it could now be seen, were trimmed with such a motley of other colors as should belong to no proper Eastern uniform.

Rolf was perhaps the first to recognize this man in black-and-motley garb, and no doubt the first to understand that Chup was pointing straight at Lisa on her rooftop. The girl had turned to face Chup; and in the lower sky beyond her, the weightless bulk of Zapranoth was turning too, like a tower of smoke caught in a shifting wind.

The Guardsmen, as Draffut approached their ranks, began shifting to and fro uncertainly, not knowing what the Beast-Lord meant to do, still unable to imagine what had called him forth. Draffut majestically ignored them; they scampered from his path, and like a moving siege-tower he passed through where their ranks had been.

Lisa on her rooftop sprang to her feet, but made no move toward Draffut or away. Her building was not occupied at the moment by either East or West, but the Eastern forces were the closer to it. Draffut after he had passed them paused briefly to set down Chup, who stood with his sword in hand and glaring at the Guard. Draffut himself strode on toward the girl. Taller than the roof he reached toward, he stretched out one mighty arm toward her—

And recoiled. Beneath Rolf's feet the ground leaped like a drumhead, beaten by the shock that had made the Lord of Beasts go staggering back.

Between the girl upon her building, and the High

Lord Draffut, there now stood one who was the tallest of the three. Seemingly sprung from nowhere, this figure was covered in dark armor, even to segmented gauntlets and closed visor. In the reflections of this metal armor, silent lightnings seemed to come and go. The world around this Dark Lord seemed askew to Rolf, and Rolf had the impression that under the Dark Lord's feet the rocks had stretched, like taut canvas bearing weights.

And in the instant of his appearance, the cloud-image of Zapranoth, that had for so long loomed above the battlefield in domination, had vanished from the sky.

Now, scattered all across the plateau, inside the citadel and out of it, bodies of fighting men let weapons rest, and held their breaths, waiting for they knew not what. Only the valkyries above still droned on imperturbably, taking up the slain and mangled and returning to find more.

Had there been listeners a kilometer away, the High Lord Draffut's voice would no doubt have reached them plainly when he spoke. "Lord of Demons, drinker of men's lives! I hear no taunting from you now. You must maintain a solid form if you will try to stop what I intend to do today—a solid form that I can grasp."

The voice of Zapranoth, even louder than Draffut's voice, began before the other had ceased. "Foul upstart beast-cub, calling yourself lord! Lord of vermin! Lord of cripples! Though it may be that I cannot end your life, you will soon wish that it had ended yesterday."

The two blurred toward each other.

Rolf did not truly see them come together, for there flashed out from their contact a moment of blind blackness to engulf him. The men around Rolf were all blinded too, if he could judge by the multitudinous outcry that sprang up. Even as the men were blinded, came the shock; Rolf once more felt it in the mountain underneath his feet, and this time in the air around him, too, more like a blow than like a noise.

He fell and blindly clutched the earth. When vision came back, it was to show men of East and West all crawling, seeking refuge, intermingled for the moment without fighting, as predator and prey seek safety from a flood upon a floating log, and keep a truce.

Rolf tried to rise, to get away, but before he could regain his feet there sounded in the voice of Zapranoth an awesome bellow of rage. With this cry the mountain lurched beneath Rolf, and its surface split like a torn garment. A fine crevice, nowhere wider than a man's body, ran faster than the eye might follow it across the walls and gardens and terraces of the citadel; in one direction it shattered the outer, battlemented wall, revealing the field before the citadel, where the army of the West had been stopped and where most of its soldiers still lay stunned; in the other direction the flying split raced up through the upper mountain, defining hidden faults by making them its path. The splitting ceased before it reached the domain of the Lord Draffut. Up there the coruscating light still flooded from an open giant's doorway, and through their smaller passages the valkyries still flew in and out.

Now when he looked back at them Rolf saw the two mighty fighters plain. The Lord of Beasts was biting down upon the armored shoulder of the Lord in Black. Draffut's drawn-back lips revealed enormous fangs, and these were sunken in. Rolf saw that wherever Draffut touched the black armor, it moved and flowed and yielded to the resistless life that poured from him. Around the demon's waist his huge beast-forearms, bright with glowing fur, were locked like mortised logs to hold and crush.

And yet the being in black seemed mightier. For all the Dark Lord showed of pain, he might have felt nothing from the bite that seemed to pierce his armor. With his own great arms Zapranoth strove to loosen the hold about his waist. He tested out one counter-grip and then another, working without haste or hesitation. At last he got both his dark-metaled hands clamped to his satisfaction upon one arm of glowing fur. If the metal of his gauntlets ran and dripped with life, he did not heed. Now Zapranoth's enormous shoulders tilted, and he strained. Slowly—very slowly—he began to win.

Rolf cried out, and bit his lip, and tried to move. Some power would not let him take a step toward the fight. He threw his sword at Zapranoth; the spinning blade vanished in midair.

Slowly—ever so slowly—Zapranoth was breaking the grip about his waist. When that was done, maintaining his own grip on Draffut's arm, he bent it farther. Draffut's jaws did not relax their bite, but through them came the muffled outcry of a titan's pain.

Rolf yelled again, and hurled a rock, and picked up another, larger one. Somehow his frenzied rage enabled him to run forward. Caring nothing now for his own fate, he tried to strike the demon with a rock. Turning in their struggle, the giants brushed him aside unnoticed. He felt an impact, and his body soaring. The ground flying up to meet him was the last part of the battle that he knew.

Chup, like all other mortal men, had been knocked down by the repeated rolling of the earth. He had continued to keep in sight the ugly young girl who clung to the swaying rooftop, her bright eyes fixed now on the giants' struggle. Then the opening crevice had split the mountain between Chup and the object of his attention. Even while the earth was still heaving like a ship's deck, Chup gathered his resolve and crossed the narrow chasm with a lunge, nearly falling into it though it was scarcely wider than his body.

Behind him he heard Draffut's muffled cry of agony, as his arm was mangled in the demon's grip. Chup did not look round. He ran on toward the building where Lisa was. Now it was so close that the roof and the girl on it were out of his field of vision.

"Will you still nurse at my shoulder, beast?" It was the roaring voice of Zapranoth. "I have no milk to yield! Bah! If I tore your arms off, no doubt you would nuzzle at me still." A brief pause. "But I can see a way to cause you greater pain than that, vile animal. All you care for is your Lake of Life. Now look! See what I do!"

Chup did not look, but jumped to grab the roof. His fingers slid on marble and he fell; when he hit the ground again, he did look back. Despite the untroubled speeches of the demon, his right arm in its armor was now hanging almost motionless, below the unrelenting pressure of Draffut's fangs. But Zapranoth's left arm was free, and with a barrel-sized armored fist he now smote down into the split that climbed the mountain. Twice he struck, a third time and a fourth. With each blow the mountain shook and rumbled; with each rumbling the crack widened by a little and lengthened generously. Draffut, his limbs broken-looking, his fur now dulled and matting, seemed helpless to do anything but cling to the demon with his jaws.

With the last blow of the demon's fist, the lengthening crevice broke into the doorway from which Draffut had come down; and with that the rumbling of the tortured mountain ended, in a sound as of a great clear bell. For a moment all was still. Then through the broken, distant doorway the Lake of Life came spurting, a flood of fiery radiance, leaping, pouring down, dazzling even in full sun.

At the draining of the lake, there came from Draffut's tight-clamped jaws a howl more terrible than anything that Chup had ever heard. Beneath the loose fur of the Beast-Lord's neck, his muscles bulged, as if he tried to tear the demon's shoulder off. Now Zapranoth, too, let out a wordless cry. Struggling as savagely as ever, the two of them rolled away, while both armies fled in panic from their path. Meanwhile the lake came down the mountain in a thin but violent stream, sliding into crevices and up from them again, leaving in its pathway rock that knew the taste of life and moved, before it sank as if reluctantly into being not-alive again.

At this latest shuddering of the earth, the building before Chup, like many others in the citadel, collapsed. The walls bulged out and crumbled almost gently, the roof caved inward with a noise that was not loud amid the greater thunders of the mountain. Chup stayed on all fours, crawling forward into the fresh ruin. He quickly found the girl, covered with dust from the masonry that had collapsed beneath her, but showing no sign of any great hurt. Sprawled on her belly on a mound of stones, she drew in gasps of air as if readying a scream. A place on her forehead bled a trickle, and she stared dazedly at Chup and past him.

A burning brazier inside the structure had been crushed, and Chup poked together its spilled coals, lighted no doubt when this day had been a peacefully chilly autumn morning. He fed in splinters from a broken beam until he had a hardy little fire. When the girl looked at him with some understanding, and began to sob, he asked: "Remember me, young Lisa?"

She only sobbed on. She moved a little, but she was still dazed.

"Don't be afraid. This will not hurt you much." He tried to hide the dagger from her with his arm as he moved it toward her head. There seemed to be no doubt where the exact place of hiding was. The dark brown mass of Lisa's hair was bound up carefully, like the hair of ten thousand other peasant girls across the countryside.

This was the girl who had appeared, seemingly from nowhere, at the house of Rolf's parents, at the same time that Charmian's sister had been left with the Lord of Demons. Rolf's people were obscure farmers, then seemingly remote and safe from wars and magic. No one searching for a hidden thing of power would have had reason to search them.

But six years passed, and war came there. By accident Tarlenot carried off the girl as he had taken others. Whatever rough disposal he might have made of her, her hair would not have been so tidily cared for. In a dream or vision the Dark Lord came, and worked hypnotically; and Tarlenot forgot his own designs, and took the girl right to the citadel. There were no more safe farms; Zapranoth would hide his life where he could see it, and be quick in its defense. So Lisa had been taken to serve a sister who did not know her because both of their minds had been altered by the demon, and because the appearance of the younger girl had probably been changed as well . . .

She closed her eyes and moaned when Chup set his dagger's edge to the tough cord by which her hair was bound. When the cord parted, a feeling like the shock of combat ran up the dagger to his hand. It was the first hard evidence that he was right. Lord Draffut, he implored in silence, clamp down your bite and hold the demon occupied. Hold him but a little longer.

The dagger Draffut had given Chup was virginally sharp; he held it like a razor, and severed the first long strands. The girl came out of her daze, then, to scream and try to fight, and he reversed his grip on the dagger and clubbed her quiet with the hilt.

He dragged her limp form closer to his little fire, and laid the first of the cut hair carefully beside the flame. With proper shaving gear, or at least water, the business would have gone more smoothly. But

Chup had little inclination and no time to be squeamish; beads of blood came upwelling from the scalp as he shaved rapidly and thoroughly. The girl moaned, but did not move.

Chup noticed first a strange, deep silence all around him. But he did not look round. Then, somewhere nearby, there spoke the voice of Zapranoth, in all its power and majesty: "Little man. What do you think that you are doing there?"

Chup's hands began to shake, but without looking up or pausing he forced them to shave another swath. He could sense the power of Zapranoth above him, descending onto him—the full power of Zapranoth, whose mere passing in the cave had turned his bones to jelly. Chup sensed also that as long as he kept his full attention on his task, he could balance on a perilous point above annihilation.

"What you are doing is a nuisance to me. Cease it at once, and I will see to it that your death is quick and clean."

Once pause, at this stage of his work, and he would never work again, nor fight nor play nor love. Chup knew it by some inner warning: do not stop, look, turn. Hands that had mangled the Lord of Beasts would close upon his merely human flesh. Though Chup's own hands threatened to disobey him, he made them shave more hair and set it by the fire.

"Put down your knife and walk away." Zapranoth's voice now was not loud so much as it was overwhelming. It seemed impossible that anyone could say—or even think or hope—a word in contradiction. Chup felt his concentration slipping. In a moment he would answer, he would turn, he would face Zapranoth and die.

"Powers of the West!" he cried aloud. "Come to my help!" His hands meanwhile kept at their work.

"I am the only power who can reach you now, and

what you are doing arouses my displeasure. Put down your knife and walk away. I repeat, you shall have a clean death if you do — clean, and far in the future, after a long and pleasant life"

Lisa-Carlotta' face was changing, as the last of her hair was taken off. The ugly proportions of her nose and jaw and forehead flowed and melted into shapes of beauty, as some pressure that had steadily deformed them was removed. She whimpered, in a new and lighter voice. In spite of her dirt and her raw, oozing scalp, Chup thought he could see Charmian's sister in the unconscious face.

"Put down your knife," said Zapranoth, "or I devour you. You will join your whining Beast-Lord in my gut, where both of you can cry forever."

Chup turned, but just enough to feed a little more wood into the fire, still not looking up toward the demon. Then between thumb and finger Chup lifted a lock of Zapranoth's life from the dark brown pile beside the flame. He tried to think how Western wizards worded their spells, but he could not remember ever hearing one of them. True, it might not be necessary to say anything at all, with Zapranoth's life right in his hands. But he suspected that against such an adversary, all the help that he could get would not be too much.

In his insistent, overwhelming voice the demon said: "Far from here is a mountain that I know of, having hidden in it gold in amounts undreamed of even by Som the Dead. I see now, Chup of the North, that I have greatly underestimated you. I am prepared to bargain, to avoid the trouble you can cause me."

And Chup fed the first of Zapranoth's life into the fire, saying: *"You will fall by the flame. The knife of fire is in your head."*

The words were rather good, Chup thought, pleased at his own unexpected power of invention. From outside there came what might have been an indrawn breath, but was a sound too deep for human ears to fully register. Then Zapranoth said: "I am convinced, Lord Chup. From now on we must deal as equals."

Very good, thought Chup. What to say next?

"Your ears are cut off."

"I submit to you, Lord Chup! You are my master, and I will serve no other, so long as you permit me to survive! As good beginning to my service, let me take you to the golden mountain that I spoke of. Deeper inside it even than the vault of gold, lies buried an emerald so great—"

Chup opened his mouth and found words coming to him. *"Opening him with this knife of fire. Separating flesh—"*

The scream began in the mighty voice of Zapranoth, but ended in the shrilling of a woman. She cried out then: "Ah, mercy, master! Burn me no more. To you I must show myself in my true form." And Chup without stopping to think looked out of his ruined building, and saw a young woman stretched out on the ground, clothed scantily in her own long hair of fiery red, and in her one body she was all the women he had ever yearned to have, yes, Charmian among them. To Chup she stretched out her imploring arms. "Ah, spare me, lord!"

He craved no more the gold and emeralds of the East, but this temptation could have moved him. Still, he knew better than to heed another lie. He burned more hair.

"Separating flesh, piercing hide. I give him to the flames."

The woman screamed again, and in mid-scream her voice belonged to something else, surely nothing human, and surely not the powerful Lord of Demons; but yet it was Zapranoth's. With shaking hands Chup fed more hair into the crackling flame. He was somehow making up the words he needed, or they were being sent to him.

"In the name of Ardneh—"

Where had that name come from? Where had he heard it, before now?

"In the name of He-Who-Wields-The-Lightning, Breaker of Citadels,

I fetter Zapranoth.
I fetter him with metal.
I make his members
So that he cannot struggle.
I force him to vomit what is in his stomach."

Chup looked outside. The image of the woman was gone, and in its place lay something huge, that made Chup think of greasy ashes, and of a mound of corpses on a field of war. The thing was fettered in mighty hoops of shining metal, and the labored breathing of it sounded like the wind. The greasy ashes stirred and struggled, made heads and tails and many-jointed limbs, but could not get from out the binding bands. And now a mouth larger than any of the others appeared, yawning as if forced open from inside, and from it there tumbled forth all manner of wretched people and beasts. The people wore the clothes of many lands, or none at all, and rolled about and lay stunned and crying like new-born babes, though most of them were grown. Among them were some soldiers of the West, their weapons still in hand. And there was one huge figure, that Chup recognized . . .

Tumbling back to life from what had seemed the bitterest of nightmares, the High Lord Draffut gave no immediate thought to his own condition, or to the outcome of the battle, or to anything except the ruin of his lake. Disregarding the ruin and confusion that surrounded him, he raised his eyes at once to what had been his high domain. The radiant cascade of the lake had slowed to a mere trickle. It was draining with the new finality of death.

He rushed at once to climb the slope behind the

citadel. Power remained in him to melt the rock to life, and make it form holds for his hands and feet; the power absorbed through ages of his dwelling in and near the lake, that would not let him die, that healed his bones almost as fast as they were broken. Only this life-power let him bear the shock when he had mounted to his lake and found it a drained shell, cracked at the bottom like a broken egg. The dull, black fabric of its inner lining, the only material the Old World had devised that could resist the quickening force of pure life-principle—this shell remained, now for the first time in his memory marked by no shifting patterns or gay butterflies. The healing machines, their lives already fading, hopped and struggled feebly, like dying frogs in a drained pond.

Draffut did not stand long within the broken doorway, gazing at the utter ruin of his life and purpose. The cries from down the slope came to his ears. Human cries, from the battlefield, of men in deadly need and fear. He moved to answer them, without stopping to consider what he might be able to do.

Down the slope again he went, walking at first, then quickening his strides into a run. Before him like a trodden anthill lay the demolished citadel and its swarming men. Here and there they were still fighting one another. But there were no more valkyries in the air.

Close before Draffut one of them lay motionless, smashed by a fall, rotors bent and body broken with the violence of its crash. A look through the sprung-open belly doors showed Draffut that the man inside was cold and dead. Draffut, raging, picked up the machine, shook it and shouted at it. Where his hands touched the metal it stirred with faint life; but that was all. Only now did the magnitude of what had happened come home to the Lord Draffut with full force. Even if he could somehow repair or vivify this machine, there was nowhere for it to go, no healing possible for the dead man inside. Nor for any of the others who now lay upon the field, or who might fall tomorrow.

Far down the mountainside, near where the great crack in the mountain had shattered the citadel's outer wall, a bright gleam caught Lord Draffut's eye. It was the many-colored radiance of the lake, trapped in a small pool in the rocks. At once he tore the battered flyer apart, pulled out the corpse inside. Cradling the body tenderly in one arm, he hurried on.

Reaching the small pool, not much bigger than a bathub, he found that some of the wounded of both armies had sought it out already, were sprawled beside it drinking, or splashing the fluid on their wounds. Picking his way carefully among these injured men, Lord Draffut reached a spot beside the radiant pool. He dropped into it the dead man he carried, then set himself to disperse healing to as many as he could.

With every passing moment, more wounded, mostly Easterners, were crawling and staggering to the place. A groaning, demanding throng grew rapidly around the Lord of Beasts. The level of the fluid in the pool sank rapidly as well—rock could not hold it in for long—and Draffut crouched low beside it, scooping up healing handfuls which he poured into mouths or onto wounds. The dead man he had carried here was sitting up and groaning now.

Draffut splashed a remnant of the lake onto a mangled arm-stump, whose owner shouted with the ending of his pain; perhaps a new and proper arm would grow. Another man, his belly opened, came sliding in blood to reach the pool, and Draffut poured for him an end of agony.

Amid the general cries of pain, and with his dazed concentration on his task, Lord Draffut did not notice when a different, heartier voice, raging and commanding, was raised in the rear of the rapidly growing throng about him.

"—back to your ranks, malingerers! The enemy still holds the field. You who can walk, rejoin your units, cowards, or I'll give you wounds . . . Guardsmen! Take up your arms and fight for me!"

Nor did Lord Draffut, in his dazed state, fully notice what was happening when this shouter came raving, scattering wounded Guardsmen from the pool with blows of the flat of his sword. Draffut was aware only of one more victim reeling toward him, with sunken eyes and the stink of terrible gangrene. Draffut scooped up for this one a generous handful, and threw it accurately. From his hand the fluid of the lake leaped out, a clear and innocent serpent in the air. Only in that instant did the sunken eyes of the raving, raging man meet those of Draffut, in a look that the Beast-Lord would long remember; and only in that instant did Draffut know who this man was.

The splash of liquid struck. A maddened shout ceased in mid-syllable, a sword dropped clanging to the ground. Then nothing more was heard or seen of Som the Dead. He and his portion of the Lake of Life had vanished from the world of men.

" —with the knife of fire I cut off feet and hands,
Shut his mouth and his lips —"
The bellowing of Zapranoth grew louder and more desperate, and at the same time became more muffled.

"Blunted his teeth,
Cut his tongue from his throat.
Thus I took away his speech,
Blinded his eyes,
Stopped his ears,
Cut his heart from its place."
The fire swam before Chup's eyes, and the

exhaustion of the magician, a feeling new to him, seemed to weaken his every bone. Once more he begged the powers of the West to send him words, for it was growing very hard to think. Then summoning his strength, he shouted:

"I made him as if he had never been!"

Silence had fallen all across the riven plateau of the battlefield; in silence the army of the East had begun to turn to desperate flight or to surrender. Looking where Zapranoth had been, Chup could see no more metal hoops, no more heap of greasy ashes, nothing.

But in his mind still spoke the Demon-Lord: Master. Yet a very little of my life remains. Save that, and from it all the rest can be remade. My powers can be restored, to raise for you an army to lead, to build for you your kingdom—

Chup with great care gathered the last hairs, while beside him Lisa-Carlotta moved her mistreated head and once more opened her dazed eyes.

"His name is not any more.

His children are not.

He existeth no more.

Nor his kindred.

He existeth not, nor his record;

He existeth not, nor his heir.

His egg cannot grow.

Nor is his seed raised.

It is dead.

And his spirit, and his shadow, and his magic."

Thus was the Lord of Demons, Zapranoth, destroyed, and thus did Chup of the North earn a place in the army of the West. His bride was searched for, especially where some said they had seen her pass, descending along a new path created by the splitting of the mountain. But she was not found.

When the last drops of his lake were gone, the great Beast-Lord Draffut fled to somewhere where there were no cries of wounded men.

"Lisa?" Rolf of the Broken Lands had come to

speak to the unrecognizable girl who, they said, had been his sister once.

"Rolf." She knew him, but her voice was dull. She was inconsolable—not for her own pain, not for the East's defeat, nor for any of the fallen—save one.

"My Dark Lord," she said. "My strong protector. He was all I had."